FARMER WANTS A WIFE

Skye works in London, with no intention of ever going back to the farming life in which she was raised. Then she travels to meet with Charles, a new client who lives in rural Wales. When she crashes her car in heavy snow, she is rescued by Ren and Gethin. Snowbound, she starts helping on their farm — and growing closer to Gethin. But when Skye's business with Charles threatens her new friends' livelihood, she has a hard decision to make . . .

SARAH PURDUE

FARMER WANTS A WIFE

Complete and Unabridged

LINFORD
Leicester

First published in Great Britain in 2018

First Linford Edition
published 2019

LP

A catalogue record for this book is available
from the British Library.

ISBN 978–1–4448–4007–0

Published by
F. A. Thorpe (Publishing)
Anstey, Leicestershire

Set by Words & Graphics Ltd.
Anstey, Leicestershire
Printed and bound in Great Britain by
T. J. International Ltd., Padstow, Cornwall

This book is printed on acid-free paper

1

Stormy Introduction

Skye leaned over the steering-wheel and tried to peer out of the windscreen. The snow was coming down so fast now that the flakes seemed to have joined hands. The road was covered in a thick carpet of snow, making the whole landscape one big blur.

Skye had slowed the car down to a crawl but still could feel the tyres slip and slide. She knew she should have stopped and waited out the storm but the prospect of a night in the car didn't appeal. She had thought to bring a blanket but even in her warmest ski jacket, the cold was eating into her bones.

No, she need to keep going, even if she was driving slower than she could walk. She had to get to The Manor. The account was too important, the client was too important. It didn't matter if she got snowed in once she got there. In fact, if she did, it would probably be a bonus. More time to convince Charles Raleigh that Skye's PR and Event Management Company was his best choice.

Her mind wandered as she imagined being in charge of all the events at the former castle, which had been converted into a luxury hotel, spa and conference centre. She could see herself in designer clothes, welcoming the rich and famous to another 'not to be missed' party.

Just as she was mentally shoe shopping in London's exclusive Regent Street, the back of the car started to move independently to the front of the car and Skye could feel the world around her start to spin. Considering she was crawling along, the spin seemed to be getting quicker.

A strong gust of wind whipped up the snow and for a split second, Skye could see that the road was heading down into a deep dip that could easily be classified as a black run, in skiing terms. Without thinking what she was doing, she stamped on the brakes in her hire car. It was a low-to-the-ground sports car that she had decided would impress Mr Raleigh, but she was now regretting her choice.

Braking had no impact on her forward momentum; she only succeeded in making the car spin and skid even more. It was difficult to tell but she was pretty sure she was now heading down the hill sideways. With each passing second, the car seemed to be picking up speed and all Skye could think to do was close her eyes and wait for the impact.

When it came, it was a bit like driving sideways into a wall. The passenger side took the brunt of the impact but it was enough to make Skye hurtle first forward and then backwards, her head colliding painfully with the side window.

The engine stalled and the lights dimmed and Skye was surrounded by blackness. She sat staring at nothing in the darkness for some time, she wasn't sure how long. Her body was starting to send her messages: her head ached but she could move and feel all four limbs.

The wind was roaring outside but there was another noise, like a deep rumbling roar and Skye wondered if it was a monster, come to finish off a truly dreadful day which had started out with so much promise. The noise grew louder and louder and Skye put her hands over her ears.

There was movement outside but the snow was too thick to make out clearly what it was. Whatever it was, it was huge and furry.

The sudden blast of cold air was enough to cut through some of her brain fog. She twisted her head up and looked into the monster's face. Except it wasn't a monster, it was a man, an extremely tall man, with a grizzled

4

beard and a parka jacket with the hood pulled up.

'Miss, are you all right?' the gravelly voice asked in a deep Welsh lilt. He sounded concerned and friendly.

A light, too bright after the darkness, filled the car. Skye held up a hand to try to block out the brightness.

'What on earth is she doing out here, in this?' This voice also sounded Welsh but a lot less friendly.

'We need to get her into the warm,' the gravelly voice said and Skye felt him lean across her. 'I'm just going to release your seatbelt, miss, then we can get you out of here.'

Skye nodded and found herself gently lifted into the arms of the tall man.

'Gethin, see if you can get her belongings.'

'Da, we need to get out to the sheep.'

'Would you prefer that we just leave her out here?' The gravelly voice seemed both amused and pointed.

The younger voice said something

which sounded like a grumble, but Skye was aware that it was making its way round to the boot of the car.

'We don't have room for all this!' Gethin said indignantly.

'You can strap it to the back. It'll be fine,' the gravelly voice said. 'Right then, miss. It's not a fine motor like yours, but we find it better in the snow.'

Skye found herself lifted gently up a step and into the cab of a tractor. She forced her eyes open and could see the hire car, half buried in snow, as the man called Gethin struggled to carry her two suitcases back to the tractor.

'I'm Renfrew, but most people call me Ren,' the gravelly voiced man said with a kind smile. 'And that's my boy, Gethin. He's not normally so inhospitable but we have some sheep up on the hill that we need to bring down to shelter.'

'I'm sorry . . . ' Skye started to say but Ren waved the comments away.

'I've lived in these hills all my life and never known the weather this bad so early in the season. You couldn't be expected to predict it, love. Now, what's your name?' His smile was warm and Skye smiled back her thanks.

'Skye, Skye MacKenzie.'

'Nice to meet you, Skye MacKenzie, although you could have picked a better evening for your first visit.'

'I've lashed the bags to the back. Now can we get back to finding our sheep?' Gethin's voice cut through any response that Skye might have made.

'Once we have dropped off our guest at the farmhouse,' Ren said in a voice that brooked no argument. He climbed up beside Skye, settled himself behind the wheel and drove the tractor into a space which Skye assumed was a field, then turned the tractor around.

Gethin had climbed up on to Skye's side of the tractor and it was clear that she was sitting in his seat. His expression was dark and Skye tried to move closer to Ren to see if she could make room for Gethin in the cab.

Gethin seemed to notice what Skye was trying to do.

'Don't bother,' he said gruffly, the first words he'd directed at her.

She tried not to roll her eyes. Clearly Gethin was going to make a big thing about this and no effort on her part was going to remove the scowl from his face as he gripped the handhold over the door.

They travelled what Skye guessed was several miles and then seemed to cut across country. Skye peered out into the gloom and could eventually make out the dim lights of a low farmhouse.

Ren pulled the tractor up in front.

'I don't like to leave you but we must go and find our stock.'

'Please don't apologise. Thank you for rescuing me,' Skye said as Gethin climbed down from the tractor.

Skye thought he might offer her a hand down the slippery step but instead he walked around to the back of the tractor and untied her luggage before dumping it unceremoniously on the small bank of snow at the front door.

'Door's open,' Gethin said before climbing back into the cab of the tractor.

Skye didn't wait to see them off. She had lost all feeling in her fingers and toes and all she could think of was getting into the warm.

She pushed open the front door, which as promised was not locked, before turning and dragging her two suitcases into the small hall. To her right was a light source and so she pushed the door open and found herself in an old-style kitchen. The fire in the grate was crackling cheerfully and in front of it was an old dog bed, but Skye could see no sign of its inhabitant.

She scanned the room looking for a kettle but there were no signs of any modern appliances. Her gaze settled on the Aga, which looked as old as the stone building, and the blackened kettle that sat on one of its cold plates.

She filled the kettle and moved it to

the hot plate. She was desperate for something to warm her insides.

There was a rocking chair by the fireplace, with a hand knitted blanket thrown across it. Skye sank into the chair and pulled the blanket around her.

The next thing Skye knew, there was a shadow standing over her. She tensed, not sure where she was or what threat the shadow might cause. Her brain seemed unable to work out what was the last thing she could remember.

She heard the sound of booted feet crossing a stone floor and then a crash of metal followed by a curse.

'She's let the kettle boil dry!'

Skye sat bolt upright, everything coming back to her in a flash. She looked up into one gentle, smiling face and one scowling down at her.

2

Childhood Reminders

'I'm sorry,' Skye said, attempting to scramble out of the rocking-chair, which had clearly rocked her to sleep. 'I was making a hot drink but I must have . . . ' Her voice trailed off when she caught Gethin's dark expression. A hand reached out to stop her rising.

'Sit down, love. Gethin here is perfectly capable of making us all a cup of tea.'

Gethin moved off to the Aga, grumbling under his breath.

'Don't you worry about him. His sour behaviour has nothing to do with you.'

Skye looked up at Ren's smiling face but saw there was tightness around his eyes which told her that he was feeling sorrow, too.

11

'The sheep?'

'All safely in the barn, bar one. And for that we can't complain, considering how quickly the weather came in.'

'I'm sorry,' Skye said again. Perhaps if they hadn't stopped for her, they could have rescued all of their sheep.

Ren waved the comment away.

'Mayhap she's found a place to hide for the night. We'll go back out at first light.'

Somehow it didn't make Skye feel any better. Ren moved to an ancient biscuit tin and placed it on the long, rough, wooden table. Skye stood up and moved to help Gethin carry the mugs of tea to the table.

'Let me,' Skye said, trying out a smile that wasn't returned.

'I think I can manage, thanks.' Gethin's reply showed he was in no danger of thawing out any time soon.

'Look, I'm sorry about the sheep,' Skye said but Gethin just looked at her as if she had suddenly grown two heads and dumped two mugs down on the table so hard that the contents slopped over the side. Ren gave his son a look, but said nothing.

'I'm worn out,' Gethin said and then strode from the room.

Skye stood where she was, not knowing what to say or do.

'Come sit. Ignore the boy — you just reminded him of someone, that's all.'

Skye slid on to the bench opposite Ren and cradled her mug of tea, the warmth feeling good in her hands.

'An old girlfriend?' Skye said, more to herself than anyone else. Surely only an ex could inspire that level of venom.

'My wife,' Ren said taking a slow sip of tea. 'We lost her two winters back.'

'I'm so sorry,' Skye said, feeling like she couldn't get anything right today, before glancing at the carriage clock that sat on the mantel over the fire and realising that it was no longer 'today'.

'Thank you. She was a fine woman and she is sorely missed. She used to sit in that chair and wait up for us when we had to go out at night.' Ren indicated the rocking chair with a tilt of his head.

Skye closed her eyes at her own unintended faux pas.

'No wonder he was upset. I'm sorry.'

Ren shrugged.

'You weren't to know, but I have to admit when we walked through the door for a moment I thought she had come back to us.'

Skye stared into her cup and wished she was anywhere but here. Up to this point it had been a rough 24 hours but now she had caused her rescuers untold pain. Even though Ren was looking at her warmly he was obviously a little shaken.

'I seem to have added trouble to an already difficult day,' Skye said, wondering if there was anything she could do to repay them for their help.

'Don't be daft. I'm glad we were there to help. We don't get too many visitors in this part of the world.' There was an unspoken question in the air, that Ren seemed too polite to ask.

'I'm visiting The Manor, the big castle conversion.'

'I know it,' Ren said but his tone had lost some of its warmth. 'If I was you I wouldn't go mentioning the place to young Gethin. It won't help improve his mood.'

Skye tried to think why this would upset Gethin but could come up with nothing. Her body and mind were desperate to lie down and sleep.

'If you're done with your tea I'll take you to the spare room. It's not up to The Manor's standard but I'm told it's charmingly rustic.' Now Ren had a twinkle in his eye and Skye smiled up at him.

'Thank you so much for letting me stay. I can't thank you enough.'

'Well, hospitality may not be a big thing in the place where you're from but round here, it's just how it is. We help each other out, like.'

Ren led Skye back into the hallway and up the narrow staircase.

'The upstairs is much newer than the

downstairs. Downstairs was just two rooms, which, when my dad was a lad, they used to share with the sheep.' Ren's tone was soft and it was clear that he had a great affection for his home.

'My dad had the upstairs built when he took over. He said he didn't want his children having to share a bed with the chickens.'

'It's a beautiful home,' Skye said and she meant it. Not that she would ever want to live somewhere this remote, not again, but she could appreciate its history and the place it had in Ren's heart.

'We're rather fond of it,' Ren said but Skye thought she could detect the return of sorrow in his voice. 'Hasn't been the same since my wife passed though.'

Skye nodded. She didn't know what to say that wouldn't sound trite.

Ren stopped outside a door at the far end of the corridor.

'Banon always kept this made up and you should find anything you need in the drawers. Help yourself. Bathroom is next door. I'll let you sort yourself out first. Sleep well.'

Skye watched him walk to the other end of the corridor and push open the door. It reminded her so much of her old home that her heart clenched in her chest.

In the middle of the room was an old brass bedstead, covered in sheets and homemade blankets. The walls were papered with a tiny rosebud print which was reflected in the thin curtains that hung at the small windows. A chest of drawers, stained and worn and obviously a family heirloom, sat against one wall. By the bed was a single wooden chair holding a bedside lamp and a wind-up alarm clock.

On one side of the bed were her suitcases, that she suspected Gethin had brought upstairs, probably not to be kind but to get them out of the way. He had dumped them right inside the front door.

She went over and opened the first

one, pulling out her pyjamas. They were silky and entirely unsuited to the room which seemed to have no source of heat. She delved through her suitcase for more layers but found nothing appropriate.

Remembering Ren's words, she turned her attention to the chest of drawers and pulled open the top drawer. Inside she found a woollen jumper and some wool socks which she quickly pulled on before grabbing her toiletry bag and padding along to the bathroom.

Skye didn't take long freshening up, before creeping back to her room. She pulled the curtains across the windows, before slipping under the covers and pulling them up over her head, as she had so many times in her childhood.

3

An Unexpected Find

When Skye woke up she felt like she had travelled back in time. Overnight she had wriggled down to the very end of the bed, with the covers pulled tight over her head. She couldn't tell what time it was and so tried to pull the covers down but found that they wouldn't budge.

As she reached out to each side of her, she found two solid objects weighing down the covers. For a few seconds, she lay very still. Perhaps she had been sleepwalking and climbed into someone else's bed? She had never done that before but after the events of the day before, she wouldn't have been surprised.

Now she came to think of it, that didn't explain the weights on both sides of her. Skye could feel her senses return and knew she was being ridiculous. If she had somehow climbed into the wrong bed, she was sure the occupant or occupants would have noticed.

With her arms by her side, she did a funny shuffle up the bed and reached the top, her head breaking through the heaviness of the covers, and was dazzled by white light. The curtains weren't lined and it seemed the sun had decided to put in an appearance, but somehow Skye knew that the brightness and the muffled air meant that the snow had settled and was lying deep outside.

Her eyes started to adjust to the light and looking down, she could now see the two things that had weighed her down. Two collie dogs lay stretched out on the bed, on each side. One had some grey hairs around its muzzle but other than that, they were almost identical.

'Hello, you two,' Skye said, wriggling some more so that she was sitting up and could reach out and give them each a stroke. The dog without the grey opened one eye and Skye could have sworn that he or she was grinning. He padded up the bed to give her a good-morning kiss.

Skye couldn't help laughing. She had always had dogs when she was growing up but what with the hours her job required, and the tiny flat she shared with a friend who wasn't keen, she hadn't had a pet for several years.

The grey-muzzled dog grumbled but Skye got the distinct feeling his complaints were aimed at the younger dog, who seemed to shrug but then carry on licking Skye's face.

'Should you be in here? Not that you aren't welcome. It's nice to have such a warm greeting.'

The memories from the day before, and more importantly from last night, were starting to form a kind of order in Skye's mind and with them came a sense of the awkward encounter that she knew she would have to get through before she could leave.

Gethin had made it quite clear that he didn't want her here and she had done nothing to change his mind, upsetting him even more by sitting in his mother's chair.

'Let's go see who's about, shall we?' Skye said, moving the younger dog out of the way so that she could put her feet to the floor.

As she walked past her bag, she grabbed her mobile and the younger dog followed her. The older dog simply sighed, rolled over and went back to sleep. Apparently, he wasn't going anywhere.

The bedroom doors were all open but Skye didn't want to risk a peek, so she walked past them and down the stairs.

'Hello?' Skye called but there was no reply. She walked into the kitchen and saw a piece of paper propped up against the jar of locally made marmalade.

We are out to work. Will be back in time for lunch. Help yourself to anything you need. Ren.

Skye looked at her phone and realised it was nearly 10 o'clock in the morning. She couldn't remember the last time she had slept so late and for the first time in a while she felt almost refreshed, aside from the faint pounding in her head.

She felt her scalp and there was a lump where she had hit her head on the side window. What she needed was a cup of coffee, maybe something to eat and then she would need to start making phone calls.

With a steaming mug of coffee and some toast with marmalade on a plate in front of her, Skye picked up her phone again. Staring at the screen she realised that she didn't have any of the bars that represented her signal. She held her hand above her head but the signal bars remained stubbornly blank.

Ten minutes later, having tried every conceivable point in the house, including hanging out of her bedroom window, she knew she was out of luck. Either she was too far away from a phone mast or the mast had been damaged in the recent storm. Either way, she wasn't going to be making any phone calls on her mobile any time soon.

She searched the house for a landline, without success, and there was no sign of any internet, either. With a sigh, she sank back down on to the bench in the kitchen and sipped at her coffee.

Skye needed to let work know where she was and she had to contact Mr Raleigh as soon as possible. She stood up from the table and walked over to the kitchen window. All of the outbuildings were covered in a heavy layer of snow.

She could see tractor marks leading out through the gate at the far end of the farmyard but it was clear that walking would be difficult, since the snow looked at least a couple of feet deep and she hadn't brought any footwear that would cope with that.

The young dog followed her back up

the stairs, acting true to character as a sheepdog, herding her and generally getting in the way. There was no shower in the bathroom so she had a quick bath and pulled on her jeans and a top. She put the jumper back on that she had slept in and padded back downstairs in search of some wellingtons.

There was a small room that seemed to be the room used to store outdoor and working clothes. Skye found a pair of boots that were only a size or two too large and pulled them on. Her conscience told her that they were most likely Banon's but she was only going to walk up the hill to see if she could pick up a signal. She would be back before Gethin could see her wearing them.

The storeroom had a door that led out to the yard and so Skye went that way, with the dog walking at her heels, or rather walking in her footsteps since the snow came up above his haunches. He didn't seem to be bothered by the cold and so Skye saw no reason not to let him tag along.

She walked around to the back of the farmhouse. The land here sloped gently upwards and then more steeply up to a rise.

It was cold but it wasn't snowing. The grey clouds above, however, looked heavy with snow and Skye had a feeling it was just waiting for the right moment to dump more of the white stuff. If she wanted to have any hope of getting away today, then she needed to make some phone calls.

The walk up to the brow of the hill was bracing and the crisp air helped to dull the throb at her right temple. The dog bounded around, enjoying jumping into fresh snow drifts and disappearing from view before frantically digging his way out.

At the top of the hill, Skye could see for miles but all she could view was white. It wasn't easy to make out roads or buildings due to the heavy coating of snow.

She looked in what she thought

would be the direction of her abandoned car but there was no sign of its distinctive red paint and with a groan she wondered how much she would have to pay, firstly to retrieve it, and then get it repaired.

Skye circled the top of the hill four times and at no point did her phone pick up even a glimmer of a signal. She wasn't all that surprised but it wasn't the news that she was hoping for.

The dog seemed to think it was a game and gambolled after her as she walked, not seeming at all bothered that all they were doing was walking in a large circle. Skye reached down to ruffle his ears.

'It's no good. My phone is useless, although to be fair, when I brought it, I didn't ask how good the signal was in deepest, darkest Wales.'

The dog looked up at her and then tilted his head on one side as if he was listening out for something. His ears seemed to move like radars and before Skye could make a grab for him, he had bounded off down the hill, in the opposite direction to the farmhouse. Skye watched him go, calling and whistling. But without knowing his name it was unlikely the dog was going to simply trot back on his own.

Skye kept her eyes firmly fixed on the black and tan back that she could see almost swimming through the snow and followed. It was bad enough that she had sat in Gethin's mum's chair and she was wearing her boots, which he might be prepared to look beyond under the circumstances, but to lose what was almost certainly his dog was not something she could even consider!

The slope was slippery and more than once Skye fell down, but the snow formed a good cushion and she was able to quickly right herself without injury. The dog had started heading off in a tangent to their right but whilst she had him in sight, she wasn't gaining any ground. She only hoped it wasn't a squirrel that he was after.

'Come back!' she called, even though

she knew it was hopeless. Whatever had caught the dog's nose had him fully enthralled.

Skye reached the bottom of the hill and found herself on flatter ground. A row of trees formed the boundary to her left and she followed the dog, who had darted between the trees.

'I hope you have a good homing signal,' Skye said, not sure that she would be able to find her own way back easily.

The further into the woods that she got, the darker it became. The trees hadn't yet lost all their leaves and their boughs were heavy with snow, which blocked out most of the light.

The dog barked and Skye followed the sound. When she reached a small clearing, the dog was lying down and whining. Skye followed his eyeline and saw something moving in the bracken.

'Hello?' Skye called wondering if she wasn't the only one who had got lost. Nobody answered but there was a low bleat. Skye looked at the dog who was now back on his feet. He walked forward a few paces and then laid back down. Skye moved slowly, not wanting to startle the creature and end up in a sheep chase.

The bleating sounded a little more sorrowful as Skye moved forward. The bracken shook again and Skye squatted down.

'Hey, there,' Skye said softly, 'I think I know some people who are looking for you.'

The black face of a sheep appeared through the bracken and stared at her, all the while munching on some greenery.

'Now all we need to do is work out how we are going to get you back up that hill.'

4

No Sign of a Thaw

Sheep, Skye decided, were definitely not her thing. She eyed the animal suspiciously as it continued to munch on something green. She considered throwing it over her shoulders like shepherds from years gone by but when she tried to lift it off the ground, she realised how heavy it was. That, she thought, was not going to work.

The young dog looked up at her expectantly but had no assistance to offer. Skye wondered if it was a sheepdog in training, since it had shown no urge to move the sheep in the direction they wanted it to go.

Midday was fast approaching and Skye really wanted to be back at the farmhouse before Ren and Gethin got back. The last thing she wanted was for them to feel they needed to form another search party to look for her.

'Right,' she said to the sheep, 'we're going back home. You'd like that, wouldn't you? Go back to being with all your friends?'

The sheep's expression didn't change as she just carried on chewing away. Skye turned her attention to the dog.

'Feel like giving me a hand here, bud?' The dog sat up, head tilted to one side and looked ready.

Skye nodded slowly.

'Right, take us home, boy,' she said to the dog trying to look encouraging but the dog just sat there and waited. Probably, Skye suspected, like he was supposed to, waiting for the signal. The problem was, Skye had no idea what the signal was.

She walked a wide circle around the sheep thinking that maybe she could shepherd it in the right direction. As she got closer to the sheep's back end, it seemed to notice that she was there. With barely a glance over its shoulder, it ran in the wrong direction.

'No, no, come back!' Skye shouted.

That clearly wasn't the right command either because the dog was now looking at her curiously as if he couldn't figure out what she was trying to achieve.

The dog wandered over and leaned into Skye's leg, looking up at her. She reached down and ruffled his head, feeling the collar under her hand and then the idea struck her.

Five minutes later, she had removed the dog's collar and lashed her belt to it like a lead. All she needed to do now was get the collar around the sheep.

Twenty minutes later she was hot and sweaty, despite the cold. She had chased the sheep around and almost got the collar on several times, but the sheep seemed to have a sense of when she was nearby and evaded all her efforts.

Skye found a stump and sat down. This day was beginning to pan out like the day before and that was not a cheerful thought. The dog rested his head in Skye's lap.

'Any time you feel like helping, you just step in,' Skye said to him but couldn't resist scratching him behind the ears before nodding her head in the direction of the sheep.

His ears perked up and he ran around behind the sheep and laid down. The sheep cast one eye in his direction but carried on munching. Skye took a deep breath and walked towards the sheep.

It looked like it was going to bolt but the dog cut it off. After a few false starts, Skye managed to get the makeshift collar around the sheep's neck.

'Right, come on then,' she said and tugged on the lead.

The sheep did the equivalent of digging in its heels. Skye for her part didn't want to tug too hard on the collar but the dog seemed to have finally got the gist of what was going on and moved behind the sheep, who bleated a loud complaint but moved, for the first time, in the right direction.

It was very stop-start progress but at least they were making headway. By the time the little band had made their way out of the woods, the sky was dark and threatening. It looked like there was a lot more snow about to fall. Skye looked up and then back at the dog. They seemed finally to be in tune and as she tugged on the lead, the dog drove the sheep a little faster. Even the sheep seemed to have got the message and soon they were half trotting back up the steep hill.

It wasn't easy going, for any of them. The hill was steep and the snow deep, but they finally settled into a line, with Skye clearing the way and the sheep and dog following behind in single file. They made it to the top of the hill as the first flakes started to fall and all three seemed to think that the best thing to do was hurry home. Even the sheep was managing a swift jog.

They made it back to the farmyard

just as the tractor pulled in with a bale of hay on the back. Ren and Gethin stared as Skye, the sheep on a lead and then the young dog jogged into view.

Ren was the first to find his senses and he leaped from the tractor cab to greet them.

'Skye! What on earth?' he said but he was chuckling at the same time.

'I walked up the hill to try to get a phone signal and your dog decided to accompany me. He must have picked up the sheep's scent because before I knew it we were on a sheep hunt.'

Gethin had joined them now and Skye saw a different look in his eye. He looked almost impressed. Then, in the blink of an eye, the same slightly annoyed expression was back.

'We don't let the dogs out in weather like this,' Gethin said, standing so the sheep was between his knees and removing the collar and belt.

'Hush, Gethin. With this one back, all our sheep are safe and sound. Put her in the barn for now.'

Gethin firmly held the sheep and moved off to one of the outbuildings.

'I think we all deserve a cup of something hot,' Ren said and led the way to the front door.

He busied himself filling the kettle and adding some wood to the Aga. The older dog appeared and seemed to be telling off the younger dog for going outside.

Ren laughed.

'He's the dad, Gawain,' Ren said, nodding in the older dog's direction. 'Just reminding Bryn who's boss.'

Bryn seemed to accept his telling off and then trotted over to sit by Skye's side. He leaned in and she reached down to scratch his ears.

'I'm glad Bryn was with me. I doubt the sheep and I would have ever come to an understanding without him.'

'He's a slow learner but he's getting there,' Ren said fondly, placing a hot cup of tea in front of Skye. 'Don't suppose you had much luck with your phone?'

Skye shook her head.

'I really need to let my office know I'm OK, not to mention the client I'm supposed to be meeting.'

Skye's eyes strayed to the kitchen window. The snow was falling thick and fast now.

'We don't have a phone but I know someone who does.'

'You do?' Skye's hope peaked and then dropped again. 'But I don't suppose we can get to them in this weather.'

'Probably not a good idea but that doesn't mean they can't help you out.'

Skye gave him a questioning look.

'We may be out in the middle of nowhere, but we have ways and means.' Ren stood up, holding his cup of tea and walked out of the kitchen.

Skye got up to follow him, just as the front door opened, letting in an icy blast and Gethin, who was now covered in a layer of snow.

'Tea's in the pot, son,' Ren called but kept walking.

Skye followed him and he opened a door that led down to the basement.

The room smelled dank and was lit by a single light bulb. It was like a museum. There were so many things piled up from ages past that Skye couldn't help but stare with fascination.

'We're not so good at throwing things out,' Ren said a little ruefully. 'You never know when you might need some of it and no point buying new when you don't have to.'

Skye smiled. Ren's face was briefly replaced by an image from her past but she pushed it down, she didn't want to think about it. There were too many reminders around as it was.

There was the ruffle of heavy plastic sheeting which Ren was removing from an old wooden desk. On top of the desk was electrical equipment that would not have looked out of place in the 1950s. A thick wire ran from the back of one of the metal boxes and up the wall, through the ceiling of the basement.

Ren sat down at the desk and

switched on the box, which started to hum.

'Takes a few minutes to warm up.' He handed Skye a pad of paper and a pen. 'If you write down your office number and who to speak with, Lewis will pass on your message.'

Skye took the pad and pen but wasn't sure what was going on. Ren saw her expression and laughed.

'I don't suppose you've ever seen one of these?' Skye shook her head. 'It's a CB radio. Most of the farmers round here have them. More reliable than the phone lines. Lewis lives nearer civilisation and so has a phone and one of them modern things.'

'Modem?' Skye asked with a smile back.

'Aye, that's the one. Don't see the point meself but there's been more than one occasion that we've been glad of it. Lewis calls the doctor and the vet for us. He's usually by his set. His legs don't work as well as they used to.'

Ren rubbed absentmindedly at his

right knee, and Skye suspected that Lewis wasn't the only one with leg trouble.

She scribbled down the office number and Fran's name before handing it back to Ren.

'Could you ask Lewis to say that I'm safe but I won't be getting to The Manor today?'

'I doubt you'll make it tomorrow, either.' The hum from the metal box grew louder and Ren pulled on a set of ancient Bakelite headphones, moving a few of the dials in a practised manner. When he started to speak, it shouldn't have surprised Skye to hear that he was speaking in Welsh.

His voice lifted and fell in the sing-song nature of the Welsh language and Skye listened, fascinated, despite the fact that she had no idea what was being said.

'Lewis says the weather is set for the next three days at least,' Ren said.

Skye nodded. This was not good news but then, on the plus side, it was unlikely that Raleigh would be able to get away from The Manor either. So she was still in with a chance, as long as she could get there as soon as was humanly possible.

'He's spoken to your lady and she is going to contact the client.' Ren smiled.

'Then I guess it looks like you are stuck with me for a few more days,' Skye said. She knew Ren didn't mind but she doubted that his son would share his enthusiasm.

'You're welcome to stay as long as you need to, love. We don't have too many visitors and it's good for Gethin to have more than me to talk to.'

Skye raised an eyebrow and the expression wasn't lost on Ren.

'Don't mind him, he's just passionate about the farm, that's all. It's in our blood, but I keep telling him he needs to think about life after I'm gone.'

Skye felt some of the colour drain from her face as another memory surfaced.

'Not that I'm planning on going

anywhere, mind,' he said, smiling, 'but I can't do as much as I used to. Being up in the hills only works if you have people and family to share it with.'

Skye smiled now at the lack of subtlety. Ren had as good as suggested that she might be a suitable future wife for Gethin!

But the farm represented a past that Skye had spent many years trying to escape and there was no way she would let herself be drawn back in — and that was before she considered how totally incompatible she and Gethin were.

It was laughable. He clearly could barely be in a room with her without scowling and she suspected that romance was the last thing on his mind, as it was on hers.

'Family is important,' she said, smiling, feeling like she needed to say something but not wanting to imply anything that might raise Ren's hopes, 'but I'm sure Gethin knows that and will get to it in his own time.'

Ren studied her face and Skye could

feel her cheeks start to colour.

'Well, you two must be starving. Why don't I get some lunch for you?' Skye headed back towards the kitchen, wanting to cut off any further opportunities for Ren's particular subject matter.

'You don't need to be doing that, you're our guest.'

'Well, if I am going to be staying on because of the snow, I think the least I can do is take care of the meals.'

'That's mighty kind of you,' Ren said and followed her.

Skye reached the kitchen first where Gethin was drying his hands on a towel.

'Da? Are you OK?'

Gethin pushed past her to reach his dad who, when Skye turned, she could see was limping.

'I'm fine. Don't fuss, lad,' Ren said and for the first time, Skye heard what she thought was a cross tone to his voice.

'It's your knee. Da, I told you not to

tackle those stairs! You know what the doctor said.' Gethin held his dad's arm and steered him to the wooden bench and stayed by his side as Ren eased himself into the seat.

'What did you go down there for anyway?' Gethin said, looking at his dad and then following his gaze to Skye. His expression was thunderous.

5

The Secret is Out

'I'm sure however urgent Skye's message was it could have waited for me to wash up,' Gethin said.

All of his anger was directed at Skye and she was starting to get annoyed. It wasn't as though she had insisted that Ren contact his friend straightaway. She hadn't implied it was so urgent it couldn't wait, and how was she to know that Ren wasn't supposed to be walking down the basement stairs?

Skye opened her mouth to retaliate but Ren's face was begging her not to.

'I'll be fine,' Ren said, risking a grateful smile in Skye's direction.

'You need to take some of your painkillers,' Gethin said but Ren was already shaking his head.

'They make me sleepy and we have work to do.'

'I can manage,' Gethin said, dropping his voice low and seemingly hoping that Skye wouldn't hear.

'I can help,' Skye said immediately.

Gethin's expression told her that, firstly, she had done enough already and secondly, he doubted she would be anything other than a hindrance.

'I'm stronger than I look,' she said, holding his gaze and refusing to bow to his attitude, 'and besides, I grew up on a farm.'

She hadn't meant to say it and cursed silently for letting that slip out just because Gethin, a man she barely knew, had galled her into it.

Gethin and Ren were staring at her. She knew there was nothing about her that said 'I used to be a farmer' but that was intentional. She'd spent years erasing her past.

'How about I get us some lunch?' Skye said lightly.

Ren's eyes were dancing and Skye

had to look away. She had a horrible feeling that she had just ticked another box on his 'perfect daughter-in-law' list.

She turned away and randomly opened a cupboard. In it were a mismatched selection of plates and dishes.

'There's soup in the cupboard by the sink,' Ren said.

Skye headed there without looking back and pulled out two tins of soup. She pulled at a drawer and was grateful that she had guessed right, finding in it cutlery, a wooden spoon and an old-fashioned tin opener that looked like it had been there since tin cans were invented. Her grandmother had the same style and Skye had never quite managed to master it.

She jabbed the pointed end into the first tin and started to waggle it up and down as her grandmother had, but without the same result. She could feel eyes on her back and she didn't want this to be another thing that she apparently couldn't do. She took it out again and tried another jab but this time managed to sink the sharp end into the gap between her thumb and her forefinger, rather than the tin can. Skye bit her lip to hold back her yelp but she could do nothing to disguise the spurt of blood which splattered on the work surface.

'Here,' Gethin said, seeming to magically appear at her side, 'put some pressure on it.'

He held out the tea towel and turned to the long wall cupboard which appeared to be the old pantry and came back carrying a tin box. He put the box on the table and gently led Skye to the wooden bench opposite his dad.

Skye needed no encouragement to sit down. Big black dots were forming in front of her eyes and she could feel her knees start to wobble.

'Let me see,' Gethin said, taking the tea towel away and examining the jagged cut from the base of Skye's thumb down to her palm. Skye took one look at it and swallowed before turning her head away. Ren looked suitably sympathetic.

'Looks bad,' Ren said.

'Probably could do with a stitch or two but I suspect some steri-strips and careful bandaging will hold the edges together.' Gethin reached for the tin and took the lid off, revealing a well-organised first-aid kit.

'I have been known to stitch up the sheep at a push but I'm not sure I'm ready to be let loose on a person.'

Skye was glad he was so calm but to be honest she wasn't ready to be his first human subject, either.

'Perhaps you should lie down,' Gethin said when he looked at her face.

'No, I'm fin . . . ' Skye started to say and that was it. The next thing she knew she was lying on the kitchen floor and staring up at Gethin who, meanwhile, had fixed up her hand. He placed a small clip that held the bandage in place.

'All done. How are you feeling?'

Stupid, was what Skye wanted to say.

She felt embarrassed and couldn't believe she had actually fainted. She had seen plenty of blood and guts on the farm, but somehow when it was her own, it was something else altogether.

'OK, I think,' was what she actually said out loud. With a groan she struggled to sit up. If she were in a cartoon, she knew that she would have cartoon birds flying around her head. She cautiously felt the back of her head but there was no pain and no lumps. She frowned.

'I caught you,' Gethin said, not looking at her but concentrating on clearing away the mess he had made in attending her.

'Thanks.'

Gethin shrugged.

'Not much different to delivering lambs.'

Skye stared at him but he was studiously looking anywhere but at her.

'Do you need a hand up?' he asked, replacing the lid on the first-aid tin.

'No, I'm fine,' Skye said, getting cautiously on to her knees. Her head felt foggy but otherwise she felt OK. Her hand throbbed and when she managed to get her feet underneath her, Ren waved the packet of painkillers at her.

'Welcome back,' he said. 'You had me worried there for a moment.'

Skye sat back down on the bench, not trusting her wobbly legs to hold her upright for too long.

'I'm a bit squeamish,' Skye said, which seemed like a silly thing to say since she had just amply demonstrated the fact.

'Next time, a little warning would be nice,' Gethin said, putting the first-aid tin back into the cupboard and then walking back to the tins of soup.

He picked up the tin opener and with the same smooth movement as Skye's grandmother had used, removed the lid. He made it look easy, like putting a knife through warm butter.

Skye felt both impressed and slightly irritated. Seemingly Gethin was able to do everything from farming, to first aid, to using outdated kitchen equipment.

'Hopefully there won't be a next time,' Ren said, winking at Skye.

'I'll keep my distance from the tin opener,' Skye said, trying to get a smile out of Gethin.

He looked at her as if it was just one more thing she wouldn't be able to help with.

'You must keep your hand clean and dry,' he said as he pulled a pot out of a cupboard and emptied the soup tins into it. He went behind her to the Aga and lifted the lid, then placed the pan on the hot plate.

'No problem,' Skye said, wondering how she would wash her hair but not wanting to bring that up.

The soup started to bubble as Gethin took a loaf of bread out of a ceramic bread bin. Skye got out of her seat and went to stir the soup. Gethin dumped a wooden bread board on to the table, along with the loaf and strode over to her.

He took the wooden spoon out of her hand, none too gently.

'And you need to keep it still. It really does need a couple of stitches and will only heal without them if you keep the edges together.'

Just the talk of the edges made her head swim and Skye reached out for the oven handle to steady herself.

'Why don't you sit down before you hurt yourself some more.' It wasn't a suggestion but more of a demand.

Skye did as she was told, mainly because she didn't want to give him the satisfaction of having to catch her mid-faint again.

This time she sat down next to Ren and he smiled at her conspiratorially as if he knew how she felt.

Judging by the lack of bedside manner that Gethin had just displayed, she suspected that Ren knew exactly how it was to be treated by him.

'When he's like this, it's best just to do as he says,' Ren said, clearly unconcerned as to whether Gethin would hear his words or not.

6

Gethin Goes Missing

Ren did a terrible job of hiding another yawn. They had eaten hot soup and bread and Skye felt comfortably sleepy herself.

'Da, go to bed before you fall over, too,' Gethin said, although his voice was a little softer than the tone he had used when he spoke to Skye.

Ren started to shake his head but was hijacked by another yawn.

'You can't work machinery with those pills. I'll be fine. Just go to bed, please?'

There was a wordless conversation that went on between the two men, one that Skye felt but had no idea what it was about. With a grunt, Ren pushed his chair back and hobbled to the bottom of the stairs.

Gethin hurried to follow him.

'I'm doing as you ask,' Ren said grumpily, 'no need to make me feel older than I am by escorting me up them stairs.'

Gethin stepped back into view in the kitchen doorway and Skye could see his face as he watched his dad make his way up the stairs, one at a time.

It was slow going and gave Skye the chance to study Gethin. He was tall, over six foot she would guess. His hair fell over his collar and looked like he probably cut it himself, when he could be bothered. He had the build and muscles of a man that worked the land and his hands, clenched at his sides, were rough and coarse, a testament to his profession.

Skye had been lost in her study and so didn't realise that the thumping noise on the stairs had stopped. She blinked and realised that Gethin had caught her staring.

He looked at her curiously as if he couldn't work out what she had been looking at so she looked away and started to collect up the soup bowls.

'Clean and dry, remember,' he said, indicating her bandaged hand as he took the soup bowls from her. But his tone was gentler and less judgmental.

'I can't just sit here and do nothing,' Skye said, 'it's not really in my nature.'

Gethin started to run water into the sink and dumped in the soup bowls.

'I figured as much.'

Skye picked up the bread board and carried it over to the work surface, before placing what was left of the bread in the bread bin.

'You don't like people helping you out, do you?' she asked and watched him wash up as he seemed to consider the question.

'Not when it creates more work,' he said.

'You don't even know me, so it's a bit much to assume that I can't help out a bit whilst I'm here.'

She wanted to say 'stuck here' to remind him that she hadn't chosen to stay with them, but it felt churlish after all Ren and Gethin had done for her.

'What kind of farming did you do?' Gethin asked and looked up at her.

Since he rarely made eye contact with her, Skye knew that he must really want to know the answer to the question — quite possibly the only question she didn't want to answer.

'Not me, really, my parents.'

Gethin's gaze seemed fixed on her now, as if he couldn't look away even if he wanted to. He tilted his head to one side as if she were a puzzle he was trying to figure out.

'You didn't want to follow in their footsteps?' he asked, sounding genuinely curious and it was clear that he couldn't imagine doing anything else.

'No,' she said and turned her back, returning to sit at the table so that she didn't have to see his reaction.

It wasn't true, it wasn't close to the truth. But to tell him more would only elicit sympathy and understanding — the two things that made the past so hard to bear, especially from a person who would truly understand what she had lost.

'Right,' he said as if he had decided that his first conclusions about her were right.

She was a city girl, through and through, who had no love for the countryside.

She might as well have been an alien.

A small part of her wanted to prove him wrong, to tell him what had happened. But she knew she couldn't bear to open that wound again.

As her thoughts turned to wounds, her hand started to throb and she cradled her hand in her other arm.

'I have other painkillers, if you don't want to take my dad's?' Gethin asked, obviously noticing Skye's movements.

Skye nodded and Gethin produced a packet from the same cupboard the first-aid tin lived in and handed them to her with a glass of water.

'Why don't you have a lie down, too?' Gethin said and Skye opened her mouth to argue. Whatever he thought, she was going to give him a hand, even if it meant she could only use one.

Gethin held up his hands as if he could guess what she was going to say.

'You would be doing me a favour. Da can be a little unsteady on his feet for a few hours after the pills. If you could keep an ear out for him, then I can go do what needs to be done without worrying.'

Skye couldn't tell if it was the truth or just a convenient excuse, but she had seen first-hand how he was with his dad and felt that part of his argument must be genuine. So she shrugged and left the kitchen, heading upstairs.

She collapsed on to the bed, thinking that she wasn't tired enough to sleep, and let her mind wander. Her mind seemed to decide to replay the events of the day, mainly focusing on Gethin.

She tried to focus on the preparation for her meeting with Mr Raleigh but her mind wasn't playing ball. She didn't want to think about Gethin — it was a complication that her life, the one she had worked so hard for, didn't need. So she rolled on to her side and willed herself to sleep.

★   ★   ★

When she woke, it was dark. She reached for her phone, whose glowing face told her it was past five in the evening and she had slept for hours.

Skye reached for the bedside light and turned it on, before padding over to the window and looking out.

There wasn't much to see as the snow that Lewis had predicted was falling heavily again. She listened but could hear no sounds from the house, and frowned. Surely Gethin should be back from whatever jobs he had needed to do by now?

Skye walked out into the hall. Ren's door was closed and when she listened outside it, she could hear soft snores. She headed down the stairs and did a quick sweep of the downstairs but there was no sign of Gethin.

In the kitchen, she peeked out of the curtained windows. There was no sign of the tractor and any tracks that had been left had been filled in with snow. Skye felt a tightness in her chest that spoke of worry. She tried to shake it off.

Gethin had, after all, lived here all his life and there was no reason to think he wasn't perfectly capable of looking after himself but still . . . It was late, the weather was foul and her skin prickled as if she was missing something.

She filled the kettle and wondered if she should wake Ren before deciding against it. If he was still asleep it surely meant that he needed it, or if it was the pills, waking him would mean he would be disorientated and not much help.

Skye made a cup of tea and stood at the window to drink it, staring out into the blackness, scanning the yard for any sign of lights from the tractor.

Since pacing up and down felt like a waste of energy, Skye decided to get some dinner ready for the three of them. She searched the fridge, freezer and cupboards and settled on a stew that could simmer away whilst they waited for Gethin.

Her preparations took her fifteen minutes but once it was in the Aga, there was nothing to distract her.

She returned to her post, staring out of the window and thought she could see movement — not tractor-size movement but something much smaller and faster. She stared trying to make out the shape, struggling through the snow and then she heard him.

Skye yanked open the front door. The wind had blown the snow up against the door and a small tidal wave covered the hall floor but she didn't care.

'Bryn?' she called. 'Bryn!'

She pulled on her wellingtons, switched on the porch light and waded out into the snow.

She found the dog, struggling against the snow, his whole body shivering with cold. Ice had formed on the end of the fur of his tail and his tongue lolled out as he panted.

When he saw her, he whined, and she reached into the snow to lift him up. He whined again and she couldn't tell if he was hurt or just relieved to be home and so she carried him as gently as she could into the farmhouse.

She slammed the door just as Ren hobbled down the stairs, accompanied by Gawain.

'We need to get him warm,' Skye said to Ren and carried Bryn into the kitchen before placing him gently in the bed in front of the fire.

Ren handed her a blanket and Skye draped it over the shivering dog. Gawain toddled up and started to complete his own inspection of his son. Once he had licked and nudged every part of him, he seemed satisfied and sat down next to him, acting as a sentry.

'How did he escape?' Ren asked, sounding like he was still a little out of it.

'I don't think he did. I think he went

out with Gethin.'

Ren's face crumpled in a frown as his eyes went to the window and the scene outside.

'He's not back?' Ren said, moving out to the hall and pulling on his long, padded jacket.

Skye followed him.

'Where are you going?'

'Out to find my son,' he said, reaching down for his boots and wincing.

'Stay here. I'll go.' Skye reached for her jacket and a cap that she found on one of the pegs. 'Do you have other transport?'

'There's another tractor in the shed. It's old but should do fine.'

Ren collapsed into the hall chair as he tried to get his boots on. Skye kneeled down and helped him pull them on before lacing them up. He smiled gratefully.

'Don't suppose you know how to drive a tractor?' he asked, rubbing at his knee.

'It's been a while but I'm sure it's like riding a bike.'

Gawain was standing at the front door.

'No, you don't, lad. You stay here and watch over Bryn for me.'

Gawain whined.

'We'll find him,' he said to the dog and nodded his head in the direction of the kitchen.

For a moment Skye thought Gawain would disobey but with a grumble he walked back into the kitchen and returned to playing sentry next to Bryn.

Ren opened the door and they were hit with a gust of snow. He raised his hand to protect his eyes and then stepped out into the night, with Skye close on his heels.

7

Fear in the Darkness

The snow was above their knees and Skye's jeans were quickly soaked through but she ignored the uncomfortable sensation. She had been worried herself but Ren's face told her that she was right to be concerned. Gethin should be back by now and if he wasn't, it meant that something had happened, something bad.

They made slow progress towards the shed that sat to the right of the farmhouse. The door opened inward and as they walked into the space, Ren grabbed a heavy torch which lit up the various machinery that it housed.

The light settled on a tractor that looked older than Ren himself. It was hard to tell what colour it had been. Now it was a sort of dirty brown which

Skye suspected was all rust.

Ren handed her the keys and Skye climbed up into the driver's seat. The tractor was basic and Skye inserted the key into the ignition and turned it.

The engine seemed to choke and then die. Skye looked up, anxious that she was doing something wrong.

'Pump the gas,' Ren said. 'She's stubborn but once she's going, she's reliable.'

It took four more goes to get the engine to chug into life and Skye could feel her blood pressure rise with each failure.

Gethin was out there somewhere, in trouble, she could feel it and she couldn't get a stupid tractor to start.

Ren hobbled to pull back the double height doors and Skye slipped the tractor into gear.

With her foot hard on the accelerator, which was the only way to keep the engine turning over, the tractor leaped forward and she slammed her other foot down on the brake.

Ren said nothing, just stood and watched as she eased the tractor out of the doors. Once she was clear, she waited for Ren to close the doors behind him and climb up beside her.

She shifted over in the seat to give Ren room to perch but he waved her efforts away.

He reached across her and switched on the search light lamp on the roof of the tractor and then stood, one-legged in the footwell, using the torch he had brought with him to scan the farmyard.

'Where do we start?'

Skye was trying to keep the helplessness she felt from her voice. Gethin could be anywhere.

She had no idea how much land Ren and Gethin owned but she suspected it would take some time in the snow and poor visibility to search it. Time that Gethin might not have.

She pushed the thought from her mind. It wasn't helpful. Nor was the fact that she should have insisted on going with him.

She shook her head to try and dislodge the memories.

What she needed to focus on was what was in front of her, not to mention the fact that she needed all her concentration to keep the tractor on the small lane that led away from the farm.

'We'll head up to the top barn by the main road. That's where most of the sheep are. Gethin would have gone up to feed them. If he's not there, we might be able to follow his tracks from there.'

Skye didn't like to point out how unlikely that was.

It was clear that Bryn had spent several hours at least making his way home and the snowfall was so heavy, any tracks would surely be covered by now. Instead she focused on the road, or at least what she could see of it.

The tractor's wheels bit deep but still Skye could feel the endless tug on the wheels.

She gripped the steering wheel tighter and kept the speed low. They

70

would be no good to Gethin if they got stuck somewhere out here, too.

'The road bears round to the right in a minute,' Ren said, his voice sounding loud in the muffled air.

Skye leaned forward and tried to make it out but couldn't see.

'I'll tell you when to start turning.'

Relying on Ren's directions rather than what she could see, they made slow but steady progress.

'The barn is in the top field. Keep going straight for five more minutes and then stop. We will be best to go the rest on foot.'

The five minutes felt like for ever but at Ren's direction, Skye pulled the tractor to a slow stop.

She went to turn the ignition off.

'Probably best to leave it on. It might not start and the lights will let us see our way.'

Skye nodded. Her stomach was rolling around at the prospect of what they might find, as she climbed down from the cab and followed Ren.

There were no visible tracks or footprints but Ren seemed to know where he was going.

The snow was lying thick and each footstep felt like ten.

Skye was panting trying to keep up with Ren, who seemed to be ignoring the pain in his leg, focused on reaching his son.

Ren's torch hit a solid surface and as they drew nearer, Skye could make out a huge structure made of steel and wood.

Ren slid back the bolt on the small door that sat within two large doors, and they stepped in.

The smell was the first thing that hit Skye — not surprising since the torch light was picking up on hundreds of sheep.

Seeing they had visitors, the sheep started to bleat all at once. The noise was deafening and Skye didn't realise that Ren was speaking until he tapped her on the arm.

'He's been here,' Ren said, directing

the torch to the troughs full of water and the fresh hay in all the pens.'

'Gethin?' Skye called out.

'He's not here. If he was, the door wouldn't have been bolted from the outside.'

Skye felt foolish. Of course he wasn't here. Just because she wanted him to be, didn't mean he would be.

'Where next?' Skye asked, feeling like she needed to prompt Ren out of the thoughts he seemed to be drowning in.

'He wasn't anywhere on the way here that I could see, so I think we should keep following the lane. He may have gone that way to check the hay store is secure.'

Ren was shaking his head, as though he wished he had gone with his son.

'We'll find him,' Skye said.

She spoke with a confidence she didn't particularly feel but she had to try her best to alleviate some of Ren's fear.

Back on the tractor they made their way slowly down the road, which swept down in to a low valley. The tyres seemed to be fighting for grip and Skye had to drive slower than she would have liked.

They rounded a corner and there was a flash of light.

'Stop!' Ren commanded and Skye eased down the brakes, so the tractor only skidded slowly to a stop.

Skye had seen the flash but could see nothing now.

Ren jumped down and headed off into the darkness. Skye quickly followed, her eyes scanning the dark to try and see what he had seen.

'This way!' Ren shouted and Skye hurried to catch up. Then she could see the light, shining dimly at a funny angle.

Ren ran the torch across the landscape but all they could see was snow lying over the rise and fall of the countryside.

Skye moved towards the light source, which seemed to be stuttering and at risk of going out.

'Gethin?' she called, her words

getting lost in the wind.

She held her hands to her mouth, like a sort of megaphone. 'Gethin!'

Skye turned sharply. She was sure she had heard something but was it just the wind, telling her what she wanted to hear?

'Gethin?' Skye called out again and the next minute Ren was by her side, shining his torch.

'You hear something?' he asked.

'I think so. Keep the torch like that,' she said as she stepped forward, her arms out in front of her.

The ground was uneven beneath the snow and Skye could feel her feet start to lose their grip and before she could do anything she was sliding down a steep slope on her behind.

'Skye!' she heard Ren shout.

'I'm OK,' Skye called back when she stopped moving. Cautiously, she got to her feet.

'Gethin?' she called.

'Here!' a voice came back and this time she knew it wasn't the wind.

A small pinpoint of light appeared in the distance and started to move in shaky circles.

'I'm coming!' Skye shouted and made her way through what she now figured was some kind of shallow river.

The light got a little brighter the nearer she got and it took her eyes a minute to work out exactly what she was seeing. It looked like a large lump of metal but as she got closer she realised that she was looking at the roof of the tractor, which seemed to be lying on its side.

'Gethin?' she called again and then she could see the torch and the hand holding it reaching around the roof.

Slipping and sliding on the snow and slush that filled the riverbed, she moved forward as quickly as she could.

When she finally reached him, she could see that the tractor was definitely lying on its side and Gethin was hanging half in and half out of the cab.

Her heart in her mouth, Skye crawled closer.

8

Mixed Emotions

'Are you hurt?' Skye asked, kneeling down beside him, ignoring the snow seeping in through the knees of her jeans.

'My foot,' Gethin said, shining the torch in the direction of his foot, which was jammed underneath the crumpled front of the tractor.

Skye leaned in to feel his foot and heard Gethin take a sharp intake of breath.

'It's jammed in pretty tight. I've been trying to free it with this.' He waved a metal pole in her direction. 'But I can't get the leverage I need.'

'Are you hurt anywhere else?' Skye asked, her mind going to nightmare scenarios of neck or back injuries.

'No,' Gethin said. But his teeth were

chattering and when she reached out for his cheek she could feel how cold his skin was.

She pulled off her jacket and wrapped it around him before pulling the woolly hat down over his head.

'You'll freeze,' he protested, but the chattering of his teeth seemed to have eased a little.

'Not before you will,' Skye said in a tone that brooked no argument. She took the metal pole from his gloved hand.

'I'm going to give this a go but it might hurt,' she warned.

Gethin nodded and Skye could see him bite down on his lip. She wedged the metal pole under the steering-wheel of the tractor, which had concertinaed in on itself and Gethin's foot, and tried to ignore the pain from the palm of her hand.

Using all her strength, she bore down on the metal rod and tried to ignore the grunts of pain from Gethin. But nothing gave.

Gethin seemed to know what she needed before she asked for it and handed her the torch.

'I need to climb out so I can get around the other side,' Skye said.

'Careful,' Gethin said, as Skye climbed back past him and out into the river bed.

'Do you have him?' Ren's voice carried on the wind.

'Yes. He's OK. I just need to get his foot free. Stay where you are,' she added.

The last thing she needed was Ren struggling, with his bad knee, down the bank, which would most likely result in more injuries.

She clambered over the roof of the tractor and slid down the other side. She shone the torch and used its light to place the metal pole where she thought it could do the most good. Once again, she heaved and this time was rewarded with the sound of groaning metal.

'Can you pull your foot out?' Skye

called through teeth clenched with the effort.

'A little more,' Gethin said.

Skye shifted so her body weight could push down on the metal pole. The metal groaned some more.

'Hurry!' Skye shouted, feeling her grip on the pole start to loosen.

'I'm out,' Gethin said.

Skye let go of the metal pole, gasping for breath, and climbed out of the cab. She made her way quickly back to Gethin's side.

She held the torch out to him and he shone it in the direction of his foot. Skye couldn't see any blood which she took as a good start. Gethin pulled a small knife from his pocket and handed it to her.

'My boot feels tight. Probably best to leave it on but could you cut the laces?'

Skye wielded the knife and managed to cut through the laces that were pulled tight. As gently as she could she pulled the sides of the boot apart and could see Gethin's ankle was both purple and swollen.

'I can't tell if it's broken or not,' Skye said, which was pointless since she had no idea what a broken bone looked like. 'Do you think you can stand, if I help you?' she asked dubiously. 'We need to get you in the warm.'

'It's only mild hypothermia. You really need to worry if I stop shivering.'

Skye nodded. This she knew.

She moved so that she could hook her hand under his arm. Gethin took a deep breath and then reached out for the side of the tractor, and between them they managed to get him to his feet.

He wobbled and his face was pale. Skye was scared that he was going to pass out. If he did, she had no idea how she would get him back to the other tractor. But Gethin gripped her arm tightly and after a few moments his brain seemed to adjust.

'How did you get out here?' Gethin asked as if the thought had suddenly occurred to him.

'The other tractor. Your dad is waiting with it.'

'Da drove?' Skye wasn't sure whether the tone was because he couldn't believe his dad had driven with strong painkillers in his system, or that Skye had driven.

'No, I did,' Skye said casually. 'I lived on a farm, remember? I may not know much about sheep, but tractors I've got plenty of practice with.'

Skye moved one step and Gethin hopped to join her, sucking air through his teeth.

'What sort of farming?' Gethin asked. His grip on her shoulder told her that he needed to be distracted from the pain.

'Cereals mostly. We had some animals — more for us than commercial.'

'No sheep?'

'No. We had a couple of goats.'

Gethin fell silent and Skye got the impression he was filing that information away somewhere in his head.

'Where?' he asked. 'The farm, I

mean, where was your farm?'

'On the edge of the highlands in Scotland,' Skye said, wishing they could move faster and not just because of the biting cold.

'I've heard it's breathtaking up there.'

'It is, amongst other things,' Skye said, hoping that he wouldn't ask her to explain.

'Farming is a hard life,' he said and paused in his hopping to catch his breath, which was telling of the effort it was to move.

Skye didn't need to be told that. She knew first hand and had the emotional scars to prove it, but she was grateful that he didn't push her for more.

'Is there nothing that can be done for your dad's knee?' Skye asked, hoping the change of subject wasn't too obvious.

'He needs a knee replacement,' Gethin said with effort.

Skye nodded.

'Long waiting list?' she asked.

'Stubbornness,' Gethin said. 'He

thinks I won't cope with him laid up for eight plus weeks, so he won't have it done.'

'But . . . ' Skye started to say but stopped. She was sure whatever reasoned argument she came up with, Gethin would have already used it on Ren.

'Yep,' Gethin said. He lifted his head as he spotted another light source.

'Da?' he called.

'Son, you OK?' Ren sounded anxious and Skye suspected that it had only been a huge effort that had kept him where he was.

'Ankle's bruised but otherwise I'm OK. Not so sure about the tractor, though.'

Skye knew how much equipment cost and the loss of something as vital as a tractor was not going to be easy.

'It may not be as bad as you think. I'll come back in daylight, see if we can pull it out. Maybe it can be repaired,' Skye said.

'Don't be worrying about that now.

Let's get you home and warmed up,' Ren said as he reached out for his son's hand and helped Skye ease him carefully up the bank.

The front of the tractor had prongs that were used to transport hay bales and Gethin perched on one.

'I think this is the best spot for me,' he said, gripping each side of the prong tightly. I don't think I can make it to the cab,' he said, before Ren could protest.

'It's not going to be a smooth ride,' Skye said, wishing there was another alternative, 'but I'll take it slow.'

It took almost an hour to navigate the road ahead back to the farmhouse and Skye was almost frantic with worry. Gethin must only be getting colder and she couldn't imagine how he was coping with the pain in his foot.

Finally, she pulled the tractor up in front of the farmhouse, as close as she dared and leaped down from the cab. Between her and Ren they half carried Gethin into the farmhouse.

He was quiet and didn't make any sound, which only worried Skye more. They manoeuvred him into the kitchen and sat him in the rocking chair. Ren started to pull off Gethin's outer jacket.

'Can you run upstairs and grab a change of clothes for him?' Skye was running up the stairs before the words were out of Ren's mouth.

She pushed the door open and stepped into Gethin's room. It was not what she was expecting. She had assumed it would be as simple and rustic as the rest of the house but on one wall was a TV connected to a games console and beside it sat a sound system that would not be out of place in a London apartment.

She shook her head and ran to the chest of drawers, pulling out the warmest shirt, jumper and jogging bottoms she could find.

When she had returned to the kitchen, Ren had managed to remove Gethin's clothes, which were piled in a soggy mess on the floor, and had wrapped his son up in a series of blankets. The kettle was whistling to show that it was boiling and Bryn had clambered out of bed to rest his head on Gethin's knee. Gethin was speaking softly to the dog.

Skye handed Ren the clothes.

'I'll take these,' Skye said scooping up the pile of clothes, knowing that she needed an excuse to leave the kitchen, so that Gethin could get dressed.

She took the clothes through to the room that housed their outdoor clothes and dumped them in front of the ancient top-loading washing machine. She thought about putting them through the wash but thought better of it, since there wasn't a tumble drier and the clothes would only make the room damp.

She walked slowly back to the kitchen, wanting to give Gethin enough time to dress. She walked in just as he was buttoning up a shirt. He was well built and muscular, as you would expect from a man who worked the land.

Ren was making the tea and so Skye went to inspect Gethin's foot, that was now resting in a bowl of warm water.

'How does it feel?' she asked.

'I can move my toes which would suggest it's not broken. A bad sprain.'

'That's good,' Skye said, looking up and smiling at him.

'Not really,' he said, his gruff tone back. 'It's not going to be easy to farm with both of us laid up.'

The accusing tone was back and Skye had to look away. She knew she was tired and overwhelmed by the events of the day, but she didn't want him to see the tears that had caught at the edge of her eyes.

She had just saved him but that apparently meant nothing.

'I have a casserole in the oven. You should eat something,' she said as she stepped towards the Aga, wanting to put as much distance between them as she could, whilst she fought to get her emotions in check.

9

Feels Like Home

'You're an angel,' Ren said and smiled at her, his eyes apologetic. 'We have some potatoes in the cellar. Would you mind going and fetching us some? I'll boil them up and then we can eat.'

Skye nodded and tried to smile, grateful at least that Ren didn't seem to blame her for all that had happened.

As she walked down the stairs, she knew it wasn't her fault. None of it was, but Gethin seemed to feel the need to lash out at any opportunity that he saw fit.

She searched the cellar and found a root vegetable store. She took her time selecting suitable specimens for supper, wanting to take as long as she could before she had to go back into the kitchen and face Gethin's wrath again.

She climbed the steps slowly and paused. She could hear tense voices floating from the kitchen. The dominant voice was Ren's and she felt a small satisfaction that he was telling his grown-up son off and warning him to lose the attitude.

'Da, I know what you're up to and I'm not interested. The last thing we need around here is someone who is clueless about sheep farming.'

'We both know that's not the reason you don't want her here. You have to move on, son. I won't be around for ever. Do you really want to live out your years up here all alone?'

'For starters, you're not going anywhere, old man. One bionic knee and you'll be back to your youthful self.'

Ren grunted something that Skye couldn't hear.

'And after what happened can you blame me for not being interested? Tell me if it is worse, just being us, than going through that again.'

'I want you to be happy, son,' Ren said.

'What makes you think I'm not?'

'Well, your attitude, for one. You wouldn't be pushing her away so hard if you didn't feel anything for her.'

'Have you been reading Mum's romance novels again?'

They both chuckled and Skye figured it was a safe time to return to the kitchen and act as if she hadn't heard a word.

'Potatoes,' she said, holding them in the air before making her way to the sink and starting to peel them.

Her mind was trying to take in what she had just overheard. Something, or maybe someone, had happened to Gethin and he had turned his back on any possible future relationships. She couldn't help but be curious as to what had happened to make him like he was.

Not that she was interested, of course. On that point, she could agree with Gethin. She wasn't interested in a relationship with any farmer, let alone Gethin.

Dinner was a quiet affair. Gethin seemed to have withdrawn into himself and Skye was happy not to have to talk about anything. All she could do was look out of the kitchen window and wonder whether the snow would ease up enough tomorrow for her to leave.

She risked a glance at Gethin and Ren and couldn't help but feel a stab of worry. How would they cope?

Not that it was her problem but she also knew how hard it was to manage a farm — that much she hadn't been able to forget.

'Anyone up for a movie?' Ren said and Skye jumped at the sound of his voice.

'From your collection?' Gethin asked in a tone that suggested he had seen them all many times.

Ren shrugged as if to say 'What other choice do we have?'

Skye felt Gethin's eyes skim her face and then turn to his dad.

'Why not,' he said and Skye got the distinct impression that he had decided it was the safest way forward.

After Skye had insisted on clearing up, Gethin had shrugged and hobbled off into the living-room.

She found herself sitting beside Ren on an elderly sofa. Gethin was sitting with his foot on a stool in the nearby armchair and Ren picked a movie that was in black and white on a VHS video and they all sat and watched it. Skye was surprised that she enjoyed it, cowboy movies not really being her thing, but then she had never actually watched one in her life.

'We seem to have lost one of our audience,' Ren said, nodding towards Gethin who was fast asleep.

'He's had a hard day so we should probably let him off,' Skye said. With Gethin asleep she realised that she felt more comfortable.

'That he has,' Ren said but his expression clouded with worry.

'I'm sure his ankle will be fine.' Skye

didn't add the words 'with time' but they hung in the air and she wished she could take it all back. It wasn't helpful to point out the obvious.

'It will,' Ren said, making an effort to keep his worry from his face.

'In the morning, I'll drive out and take a look at the tractor. I'm sure we can get it out of the ditch,' Skye said.

'That's kind of you, love, but you might be able to get on your way tomorrow.'

'I can do that first and, besides, didn't Lewis say the weather was set for the next few days at least?'

'He did,' Ren said thoughtfully and Skye thought she could see a twinkle return to his eye. She turned away so that he couldn't see her small smile.

He was a trier, that was for sure. If he thought he could make her and Gethin fall in love, in only a couple of days, then she ought to at least let him try.

'Do you think we should wake him?' she asked, looking at Gethin and wondering how they were going to get him upstairs.

'No, love, he's probably best sleeping in the chair.'

Ren hauled himself to his feet and hobbled over, throwing a blanket over his son and tucking him in tenderly as if he were still a small boy.

Ren took the stairs one at a time and Skye walked behind him.

'Goodnight, love. Thank you for your help today. I'm not sure what I would have done without you.'

Ren's voice wobbled with emotion and Skye walked towards him and gave him a hug. She kissed him on the cheek.

'Get some sleep,' she said. 'Our rescue mission's not done yet.'

Ren looked confused.

'We have a tractor to right, remember?'

Ren nodded, the same thoughtful expression returning to his face.

'Well, goodnight,' Skye said, not wanting to get pulled into another conversation that might end up with some reference to how perfect she would be for Gethin. She couldn't bear to make Ren sad, especially not after this difficult day.

Later in bed she tried to examine her own feelings. Despite all her best intentions, there was something familiar about the farmhouse and the farm. She would never admit it out loud, and suspected it was just the emotions of a difficult day, but it felt like home — a home she hadn't had for many years.

She rolled on to her side and tried to clear her mind but sleep wouldn't come. She finally fell asleep wondering if counting sheep would help.

★ ★ ★

Skye woke and was surprised by the light. For a moment, she thought she had fallen asleep with the bedside light on but as her eyes adjusted she realised the light was coming through the thin curtains.

She climbed out of bed and shuffled across to the window, pulling back the curtains. The world was still covered in a deep blanket of snow but the sun was shining bright in a pale blue sky.

Maybe she would be able to leave today after all. Her mind turned to the reason she had come to Wales. It was an important meeting with the biggest potential client she had ever met. If she got the deal it would mean a steady supply of work and a lot of exposure for the company. But none of that seemed to excite her. The job had lost some of its sparkle.

She heard noises from the hall and quickly dressed. They needed to go and sort out the tractor and she didn't want Gethin and Ren trying to manage by themselves, not when she was here and could help out.

Since none of her clothes were suitable she pulled on her jeans then rifled through the chest of drawers again, finding a warm shirt and another thick jumper.

97

She went downstairs.

Gethin was sitting sideways on the bench with his ankle raised and despite the sock she could see that it was very swollen.

'Morning,' she said as she walked in. Ren looked up from making the tea.

'Morning, love. Tea?'

Skye nodded.

'How's the foot?'

Gethin reached down and pulled off his sock, revealing a foot that was purple from the tips of his toes to above his ankle. His toes looked like sausages.

'Right, no work for you today, then,' she said briskly as she sat down on the opposite bench and accepted the cup of tea from Ren. 'I'll head out on the old girl and check out the tractor,' Skye said to Ren.

'We can manage. With the weather better, I expect you want to be on your way,' Gethin said, not looking at her.

'I do, but I said I would help with the tractor and I keep my word.' Skye knew she was throwing the words out like a challenge but she couldn't help it. Gethin seemed to think he had her all worked out and he couldn't be more wrong.

For starters, when she said she was going to do something, she would do it.

She looked at Gethin who shrugged, as if it made no difference to him one way or the other and Skye felt a new surge of anger. He really was the limit!

10

A Shared Mission

'I'll catch a lift with you,' Ren said, casting a dark look in his son's direction. 'If you have the time, we can sort the sheep whilst we are up there.'

'Of course, I figured as much.'

She smiled at Ren who smiled back, before walking over to the Aga.

'Full Welsh do you?' Ren asked.

He was carrying a hot plate with bacon, sausage, mushrooms, potato cakes and eggs.

'Perfect,' Skye said, deciding that focusing on Ren and ignoring Gethin, who was glaring at her over his cup of tea, was the way forward.

'Da, I don't think all three of us will fit.'

'You're not coming,' Skye said, as if

she was stating the most obvious fact in the world.

'Says who?' Gethin replied, looking like he was gearing up for a fight.

'Your foot,' Skye said, not wanting to say out loud that she would actually prefer that he didn't come.

'Doesn't stop me from coming along, any more than Da's knee would.'

Skye looked at Ren for help, who had been observing the conversation like a person watching tennis, going back and forth.

'I'm not sure that's wise, lad,' Ren said, sounding diplomatic.

'No less wise than letting you out there with your dodgy knee. I'll strap up my foot and I'll be fine. I can move my toes so it's not broken.'

Skye doubted that was the definitive way to tell, but without knowing for sure, she thought it was wise not to argue.

'I can manage without both of you.'

Gethin's look told her that he doubted as much and she could feel her temper rise again.

'Fine,' she said, trying not to sound too short tempered. 'It's your foot and your farm, but I think we can all agree that I'm the best person to drive.'

'Your hand looks like it needs a fresh bandage,' Gethin said, grabbing Skye's hand before she could pull it away.

'I can do it,' Skye said, feeling like two could play at that game.

Gethin looked for a moment as if he was going to argue but then shrugged and got to his feet.

'Give me ten minutes to freshen up and strap my foot.'

It was more of a command so Skye mimicked him by shrugging her shoulders and focused on eating her delicious breakfast.

'Gethin doesn't seem best pleased with me,' Skye said before realising that she had said it out loud and had inadvertently opened a can of worms that she had hoped to keep closed.

'His foot's paining him, that's all,' Ren replied. 'Also, he hates being laid up. Needs to feel in charge and useful, that one. Just like his mum.'

Skye didn't comment. She thought some of it might be true but felt that wasn't the full picture.

'He may not say it, but he does appreciate your help,' Ren added.

Skye looked up with her fork halfway to her mouth and raised an eyebrow.

Ren chuckled.

'He's not good at showing how he feels, is all.'

Skye laughed. From where she sat he seemed pretty good at showing exactly how he felt about her, if nothing else!

Ren took one look at her expression and laughed, too.

'What's funny?' Gethin said as he half hopped into the kitchen, holding a boot in one hand.

Ren and Skye exchanged glances and silently agreed not to share their joke.

'Skye was just telling me about how she got stuck in the snow the other night,' Ren said.

He shrugged at Skye, telling her that

it was the first thing had come to mind.

'Anyone with any sense wouldn't have been out in that weather, especially not in a car that unsuitable for the Welsh hills,' Gethin said as he managed to wedge his swollen foot into his boot.

It was so tight that he had no need to tie the laces. He placed his foot on the floor to test it out and missed another exchange of looks between Skye and Ren.

When he looked up, Skye was clearing away her breakfast things and Ren was staring at the window as if nothing had just happened.

'I'll listen into the radio for the weather. Looking at that sky we might not have all day before there's more snow, so probably best to get a move on.'

Skye nodded.

'We'll check out the tractor and sort the sheep and be back. Then maybe Lewis can put a call through for me again?'

Ren smiled.

'Aye, he'll like that. He doesn't have much opportunity to speak to folks in London.'

Ren turned his attention to his son.

'And take this with you this time?'

Ren handed Gethin an old-fashioned radio.

Gethin took the radio, looking a little sheepish, and hung the strap around his neck.

'Let me know if you get into any bother,' Ren said pointedly and Skye felt like she witnessed a glimpse of the boy that Gethin had been.

Gethin nodded and he and his dad locked eyes for a moment, before Ren gestured with a nod that they should be getting along.

Ten minutes later, with Gethin perched in the footwell, Skye was back navigating the old tractor round the country lanes.

'Yesterday would have been a lot easier if you'd had your radio.'

Skye knew that she was baiting him but couldn't help it. He was so quick to criticise her but yet he had committed one of the cardinal sins of country life . . . he had gone out by himself, without means to call for help if needed.

For a moment, she thought Gethin was going to ignore her.

'I was distracted.'

'By what?'

'By you.'

Skye bristled, feeling sure it was yet another dig at her but there was something different about Gethin this time. He still wasn't looking at her but she couldn't help but feel his reasons were now different and she wasn't sure how she felt about that.

It was definitely better that he wasn't having a go at her for no particular reason, but she had a feeling the day was going to become way more complicated than it would have, had he simply remained frosty and detached.

'Well, I should be out of your hair later today,' she said, going for an airy tone.

She watched as Gethin looked up at

the sky like the old farmers she had known as a child, and knew that he was checking out the weather. She glanced up herself but couldn't see any significant changes. The sun was still shining, not enough to melt the snow, but enough to take the edge off the chill and the sky remained pale blue and clear.

'Which way now?' Skye asked.

She knew the route but felt like moving the conversation on to safer ground.

'Left here,' Gethin said, hauling himself to his feet so that he could look ahead. 'The top barn is coming up but I suggest we go on to the tractor first.'

Skye shrugged her agreement and trundled the old girl past the turning that would lead them up to the barn.

The tractor was where they had abandoned it, lying tilted on one side in a deep ditch. Skye cut the engine to the old girl and followed Gethin to inspect it.

From what Skye could see, it was

beat up but looked like it might go if they could get it out of the ditch.

'I have some chains in the back,' Gethin said. 'I think we might be able to pull it out.' He started to walk towards the tractor and Skye put a hand on his arm.

'Let me go?' she asked.

A look crossed Gethin's face that said he might refuse but then he nodded.

'Thanks. There, in the box at the back. If you can loop the chain around the axle and then throw it up to me.'

Skye felt like pointing out this wasn't her first tractor pull but thought better of it. More often than not, showing was better than telling. She scrabbled down the back and her feet sunk into the mud at the bottom of the river bed.

With some effort, she managed to get the box open and found the length of thick steel chain. She looped it expertly around the axle and then half climbed the bank, so that she could lean up and hand the end to Gethin.

Whilst she navigated her way back to

the road, Gethin had hitched the steel chain to the front of the elderly tractor.

'You OK to drive? Just stick it in reverse and take it nice and slow. I'll watch the tractor.'

Skye climbed into the cab and turned the key. It took a few goes but she was getting the knack and soon the old girl wheezed into life. She put the tractor into reverse and started to edge back until the chain was taut.

Gethin stood in the road and waved for her to continue to reverse.

'Steady!' he shouted as the tractor righted itself, sending out a wave of muddy slush in Gethin's direction.

Skye bit the inside of her cheek to keep herself from smiling and eased out the clutch some more. Within moments the tractor was sitting upright on the road.

Gethin climbed into the tractor's cab and turned the key. There was a low whining sound but the engine didn't catch. He tried again, this time bringing his hand down hard on the dash.

The engine, not sounding much healthier than the old girl, stuttered into life.

'Yes!' Gethin exclaimed.

He turned to Skye and for the first time since she had met him, she saw him smile. It looked good on him and she wondered if it was worth risking his wrath by pointing out that he should smile more often.

Gethin switched off the engine and hopped down.

'Let's sort the sheep and then come back and pick up Boris.'

She raised an eyebrow.

'I was a kid and I thought he looked Russian.'

Skye smiled and climbed back into the old girl.

'Do you think you'll be able to drive him with one foot?'

'I was a short kid. I used to drive him, standing up and hopping from one pedal to the other. I'll be fine.'

'And he'll be all right left there, in the middle of the road?'

'No-one comes this way except us.'

Skye steered the old girl back up the hill to the top barn. If they carried on like this she would be at The Manor for dinner and she could start to work on getting Gethin out of her mind.

As they walked towards the barn, Skye knew that she had got her hopes up too soon. What they couldn't have seen from the road was that half of the side of the barn was missing.

11

A Rare Smile

Gethin stood stock still, clearly in shock. Skye moved around him to step over the shattered pile of wood and sheet steel that used to be the barn wall.

Some of the sheep remained in the barn, safe in their pens but the two pens nearest the door had one side missing and when Skye turned she could see a few sheep out in the field behind the barn.

'Gethin,' she said. 'Gethin!'

He seemed to shake himself and took a breath.

'We'll need to repair the wall, particularly if the weather is set to turn again.'

Skye nodded.

'Not to mention round up the stragglers.'

'They may come back of their own accord once we put the food down. But first we need to do something about this wall.'

'Should we contact your dad?'

Gethin shook his head.

'He'd only try to get up here to help us. I think we can manage and I'd rather tell him after we've sorted it.'

Skye smiled.

'I may have hidden repair skills that would surprise you.'

He didn't smile back, but then she didn't expect him to. If they couldn't fix up the barn and the weather turned, the whole flock would be at risk. It seemed miraculous none of them seemed any worse for wear.

Gethin disappeared into the barn to inspect the sheep first hand. Skye spotted some metal sheeting that would do at a push and dragged it from round the back of the barn.

'These should help,' she said when Gethin joined her outside, carrying a tin of nails and a tool box.

'If we can salvage enough wood to keep them in place,' Gethin said, starting to pile up the wood that could be reused and creating another pile of the bits that would be no use at all.

They worked steadily for what Skye was sure was several hours, but most importantly, they had constructed a wall that would keep out the worst of the weather.

'I could eat,' Skye said, her stomach rumbling on cue.

'There's a kettle and water bottles on the shelf.' Gethin pointed in the direction of the shelf. 'I'll set us up a fire. There should be some biscuits in the tin.'

Skye grabbed the supplies and by the time she had stepped back outside, Gethin had a small fire going. She didn't want to say so, but she was impressed. She handed him the kettle which she had filled with water and rested the two tin mugs on the stones that Gethin had placed to encircle the fire.

'We should probably drink up quickly and round up the rest,' Gethin said, looking up at the sky.

It didn't look particularly different to Skye but she trusted Gethin's instincts, not fancying having to navigate the road back to the farmhouse in heavy snow.

She had set her mind that she wouldn't be leaving today. As soon as she had seen the barn, she had known there was no way she could have left Gethin to shore up the shelter. The flock must be as precious as the fields had been on her family farm, and to lose them would risk ruin.

Gethin rolled over a tree trunk for them to use as a seat and eased himself on to it with his leg stretched out in front of him.

'How's your foot?' Skye asked, dropping teabags into the tin mugs and then carrying the tin of biscuits back to the makeshift bench.

'It feels like it's seizing up a bit but I suspect I've just been on my feet too long. I'll be fine,' he added, seeming to feel it was necessary to clarify that point. 'How's your hand?'

Skye's hand was wet and cold and a quick glance down told her that the bandage was soaked through. It would be obvious to Gethin that she had forgotten to change it, so she pushed her hand into her pocket.

'It's fine, healing nicely,' she said, hoping that was true.

The kettle whistled and Skye made two mugs of black tea. She cradled hers in her hands, enjoying the warmth but aware that time was not on her side, she started to sip at it despite how hot it was.

Gethin seemed used to drinking boiling hot liquid and drank his down in a few gulps.

He took a handful of biscuits from the tin and then stood up.

'Drink your tea. I'm going to grab a bucket and some feed and see if I can round up the stragglers the easy way.'

Skye sipped at her tea and watched

Gethin hop around the top field. By her reckoning there were five sheep out in the open.

Gethin shook the bucket and the sheep seemed to prick up their ears.

All but one trotted towards him and he held the bucket out so they could each have a taste, then pulled the bucket away and started to limp backwards towards the barn.

By the time Skye had finished her tea and eaten a biscuit, four of the lost sheep were back with the rest of the crowd, tucking into their lunch.

Skye walked out on to the top field and spied the lone sheep. She frowned. It was sitting down in the snow, almost invisible, save for its black face and ears. It bleated as she neared it and Skye thought it was going to make a run for it but it stayed where it was.

When Skye was within touching distance she could see why. Its right back leg was stuck out at an angle, rather than tucked underneath it and she could see a jagged cut.

Skye could hear the uneven crunch of Gethin's boots as he neared.

'This one's hurt,' she said softly, not wanting to scare the animal.

'Easy, girl,' Gethin said as he sank down to his knees and inspected the wound.

'It's not so bad,' he said to the sheep who seemed to be looking up into his face adoringly. 'Let's get you back to the barn and I'll fix you right up.'

Gethin looked back over his shoulder and Skye thought he was probably gauging the distance back to the barn and the pain in his ankle.

'I can help you carry her,' Skye said.

'Best way to carry a sheep is the old-fashioned way,' he said, turning to look at her. 'Over the shoulders, but I think I might need some help standing up.'

Gently, he reached for the sheep and the animal seemed to know that Gethin was there to help her, so didn't struggle.

He pulled her across his shoulders,

careful of her injured leg. He got his good leg underneath him and Skye steadied him with her hands as he stood up.

They made slow progress to the barn and Skye helped Gethin lower the sheep safely to the ground. The noise inside the barn had grown louder and louder, like a crowd of people at the sight of an accident, loudly wondering what had happened.

The sheep gave a single, tired bleat as Gethin shooed it into a pen.

'We've got some vet supplies, locked away in the cupboard on the wall,' Gethin said. 'Would you mind grabbing the coloured bandages, some gauze and the antiseptic?'

He grunted as he eased himself down to the ground next to the sheep.

Skye grabbed the supplies and acted as nurse as Gethin doctored the sheep's leg. He washed the wound in antiseptic, which caused the sheep to complain loudly. Then he dried off the leg and added a liberal coating of bright pink powder, before applying a bandage that looked like it was waterproof.

'Thanks,' Gethin said. 'Now we had best be heading back before the weather sets in.'

Skye helped Gethin to his feet and they walked to the small door that led to the outside. The side of the barn rattled in the wind but their temporary wall was holding strong.

Skye pushed on the door and the wind pulled it out of her hand. The snow that Gethin had predicted was falling, or trying to, and the wind was tossing it back into the air.

Skye lifted up a hand to try to shield her eyes. She could barely make out the old girl in the distance.

She felt Gethin slip his arm through hers and together they leaned into the wind and staggered towards the elderly tractor.

'You start her up, I'll clear the wheels!' Gethin's shout was dragged away by the wind but Skye could just about make out the words.

She hauled herself into the cab and offered up a prayer before turning the key in the ignition. There was nothing, not even a wheeze.

Skye pumped the accelerator, but nothing.

She tried again — still nothing.

She climbed down and unlatched the engine cover, pulling it back and peering into the engine. New tractors were beyond her skills but this engine was old enough to be familiar. It was late afternoon but the light was being blocked out by the heavy snowfall. She leaned in and tested the obvious that might have gone wrong in this weather. She pulled the gloves off her hands and her fingers told her all she needed to know — the engine had seized. And there was nothing she could do.

'We should get back to the barn.' Gethin's voice sounded in her ear and she could feel him beside her. 'If it's seized, we'll never get her started.'

'What about the other tractor?'

'Too risky,' Gethin bellowed. 'We're

better off staying put until the weather clears.'

He grabbed her hand and together they battled their way back to the shed. The wind was blowing so hard that Gethin had to use both hands to prise open the door. They hurried through and the wind blew the door shut behind them.

Gethin pulled the bolt across and Skye surveyed their temporary home.

It was warmer than outside but not exactly warm. She knew they wouldn't be able to start a fire and could only hope that Gethin and his dad had left some more supplies other than the tin of biscuits and water.

'Gethin to Da,' Gethin said, holding the radio to his mouth and then releasing the button and waiting for a reply.

'Go ahead, son.'

'The barn was damaged in the storm. Took longer than we thought to repair. The old girl won't start so we'll sit out the worst of it here at the barn.'

'You sure, son?'

'We don't have much choice. I don't fancy getting lost trying to make it on foot.'

'Understood. Keep in touch. Over.'

Skye had sat down on a bale of hay as she watched the sheep snooze and munch, wishing she could make a warm drink.

'It's not as bad as it looks,' Gethin said, almost apologetically. 'And Da and I keep a few supplies up here for emergencies.'

Gethin disappeared into the back of the barn that was walled off from the sheep pens. He limped back with two tartan blankets and what looked like a camping gas stove.

'At least we can make tea and warm up some soup.'

Skye wrapped a blanket around her knees and smiled up gratefully.

'It's not so bad. I've found myself in worse conditions.'

'Really?' Gethin said and his surprise irked her a bit.

'I did Duke of Edinburgh at school. Until you have had to camp out in a tent in weather like this, you don't know what suffering is.'

'Camping, in the snow?'

Skye shrugged.

'It was Scotland. You think it snows here, you should try the Highlands! We had to put on every item of clothing we had brought with us and huddle together until the mountain rescue team turned up.'

Gethin was working on opening a tin of soup.

'You're right — based on that story, this is practically luxurious,' he said with a small grin.

His eyes seemed to reflect the emotion and Skye was once again reminded how handsome he was when he smiled.

'Mind you, if we're stuck here overnight, sharing body heat might be an option.'

12

In His Arms

Skye tried not to read too much into Gethin's comments. She was feeling all at sea with his changing attitudes and had to remind herself of the pointed conversation they had had that morning.

She wasn't sure what had changed or whether the change would last. What she couldn't afford to do was to get drawn in.

It wasn't what she wanted and they could have no possible future, since she couldn't imagine Gethin walking away from the farm and setting up with her in London.

Whatever they decided that they might feel about each other, it would be dangerous to test it out. Only pain could result, she knew that, and suspected that he knew that, too, having overheard his conversation with his dad.

Gethin kept a regular check on the weather but there was no change. If anything it was just getting worse. By five o'clock it was dark and the snow continued to swirl in the wind. Heading out now would be crazier than if they had tried in the daylight.

'I think we're stuck here for the night,' Gethin said, struggling to pull the small door closed against the wind.

He didn't look particularly bothered and Skye knew this wasn't the first time he had been forced to camp out with the sheep.

'Better off here than stuck somewhere outside in the tractor, I guess,' Skye said, although she wasn't relishing the thought of sleeping in the barn.

'Gethin to Da,' Gethin said into the radio.

'Go ahead.'

'We're going to hole up here for the night. With luck, we'll be able to head back at first light.'

'Keep warm and try to get some sleep. Over.'

Gethin turned to Skye.

'Right, time for us to make a makeshift bed.'

Skye realised he had said bed, singular, but thought it was a bit much to insist on separate beds in the circumstances. Gethin started to pull bales of hay to form a small 'room', and then broke up one bale and scattered it across the floor.

He went back behind the partition and came back with empty sacks that had been used for the sheep food. He handed them to Skye and she arranged them over the hay 'mattress'.

Gethin returned with a couple of lanterns that were battery powered and set them on the hay bales so that they could see more clearly in the gloom.

'Supper is going to be much the same as our late lunch,' Gethin said apologetically. 'I have a couple more tins of soup and I found some hot chocolate.'

Gethin dumped his find on to the hay bales. They ate supper sitting crossed-legged on their makeshift bed and Skye had to admit that it had a surprisingly cosy feel.

Gethin had put out some more hay for the sheep and the flock seemed content to quietly munch away, with only the odd 'baa' to disturb the relative peace.

'We should probably try to get some sleep,' Gethin said. 'I'd like to get out to the tractor at first light if we can.'

Skye nodded as she wiggled down on the makeshift bed and pulled the blanket up over her shoulders. She rolled on her side, away from Gethin, and wondered if she would be able to sleep at all.

The sheep seemed to have settled into a low murmur of baa-ing and it was warmer in the shed than she expected, but having Gethin so close was more than a distraction.

His change in attitude was confusing and she had no idea what her own heart was doing, but at the very least, it was ignoring the sensible part of her brain. There was nothing for it: she needed to leave and get back to her own life. She knew once she did she would be able to remember all the reasons why even thinking about falling in love with Gethin was crazy.

Skye was stuck in a moment that she didn't want to remember. She could see her dad's face, see the anguish and how lost he was. They both knew it was over and the failure that they felt would never leave them. Her dad could barely look at her, so lost in his own pain that a gulf seemed to have formed between them.

Skye tried to reach out, tried to tell him that it would all be all right, even though she knew, deep down, that nothing would ever be the same.

As she reached out, her dad seemed to get further and further away. She was losing him and all she could do was shout out his name . . .

'It's OK,' a soft voice said and Skye

could feel arms pull her into an embrace. She could hear the steady pound of a heart in a chest.

'Daddy?' she asked, as her eyes told her that it was pitch dark.

'It's OK, I'm here,' the voice said again and Skye felt like it was OK, although she couldn't explain why. A hand rubbed her back gently and Skye felt the tug of sleep. The emotions seemed to ebb a little and the pain faded. The arms held her close and Skye felt safe, the memory of the nightmare faded and she drifted back off to sleep.

★　★　★

Skye wasn't sure what had woken her up: the noise perhaps, of 200 sheep greeting each other with the morning news or the light starting to shine through the gaps in the temporary wall. Or perhaps it was the chill wind, also finding a way through the gaps which ruffled her hair.

She tried to piece together the events of yesterday and she remembered that they had been stranded by the weather and the mechanical issues with the tractor.

Her brain registered that although the wind felt cool on one cheek, the rest of her was both warm and comfortable. Her other cheek was lying on Gethin's chest and his arms encircled her tightly.

Skye stayed still. She would never admit it to anyone, perhaps not even herself, but she felt completely at ease. It had been a long time since she had been held, had felt like she had a protector, and she didn't want to break the spell.

She closed her eyes but the sensible part of her brain was now awake and telling her to get up. This was not what she wanted, not in the long run. She had a career and besides, the thought of going back to farming was beyond what she could bear.

Skye shifted. She didn't want to, but she knew she needed to. Gethin's attitude towards her had thawed and she didn't want to give the impression that she would be interested in him. That would be cruel, when she knew that as soon as she could, she needed to leave.

The more awake she became, the more aware she was of the ache in her hand. It was throbbing in time with her heartbeat and wiggling her fingers made the pain worse.

'Morning,' a sleepy, deep voice said.

Skye wriggled some more but Gethin didn't seem like he was planning to let go of her any time soon.

'Morning. It's light. We should probably get up,' Skye said as she felt Gethin shrug.

'We should, but this is nice. I think the sheep can hang on for their breakfast for a bit longer.'

'What about your dad?' Skye asked.

She didn't want to force him to let her go, it seemed at the very least churlish under the circumstances, but she knew that staying as they were

132

would only endanger both of their hearts.

'I'll radio him as soon as we are up,' Gethin said, shifting slightly but not releasing his grip. 'I think we can afford another ten minutes or so.'

Skye knew that he was smiling. She couldn't see his face but she could feel it. She briefly closed her eyes, knowing it was dangerous but giving into that part of her that wanted to be held.

Skye wasn't sure how long they had slept on but it was the radio that woke them.

'Da to Gethin.' Ren's voice sounded urgent and Skye suspected he had been calling them for some time.

Gethin shifted and reached an arm out for the radio. Skye took her opportunity and moved too, albeit reluctantly. She pushed back the blanket and used one of the hay bales as a lever to get herself to her feet. She could feel Gethin's eyes on her as he answered his dad.

'Gethin, here. Go ahead, Da.'

'Weather looks better, son, for this morning at least.'

Gethin dipped his head to look out at the gap. The sun was shining weakly but there was no sign of snowflakes.

'It does. We're just seeing to the sheep and then we'll see if we can get the tractor going.'

'Keep me posted.'

Whilst Gethin had been speaking to his dad, Skye was heating some hot water on the small stove and trying to ignore the throbbing in her hand. There were a few biscuits left and a couple of sachets of hot chocolate. It wasn't much of a breakfast but was better than nothing.

Gethin was moving around, laying out fresh straw for the sheep before returning to the partitioned area and hoisting a bag of feed on to his shoulder. Skye watched as he filled up each pen's food trough.

The noise level rose until all the sheep were happily eating. Skye handed Gethin a mug of hot chocolate and he smiled. Skye wasn't used to seeing that expression on his face, at least not aimed in her direction, and she turned away to grab the tin of biscuits, to give her time to get over her response. She knew she was feeling slightly giddy but didn't want that to show.

She waved the biscuit tin under his nose and he helped himself to a few. They sat on the hay bales and ate in silence but somehow it wasn't as awkward as it had been.

Gethin took a sip from his mug.

'So, do you want to tell me what last night was about?'

13

No Going Back

Skye looked down into her mug. She didn't want to talk about it. She didn't want to invite the memories back. Not of Gethin holding her — those she would happily relive — but of the nightmare itself.

'Not really.'

She peeked up from her study of her hot chocolate and could see that he was gazing at her and all she could see in his expression was understanding.

'I get it. I haven't really spoken about my mum, not even to Da. Too painful.' Now it was Gethin's turn to avoid looking at Skye.

'I don't think anything can prepare you for the loss of a parent.' Skye could feel her heart contract in her chest but there was less of the hollow loneliness that usually came with the sensation.

Gethin stood up and crossed the makeshift bed and sat beside her on her hay bale. He said nothing but his closeness was a comfort.

'Mum was such an amazing person. She was so full of life, even at the end . . . ' His voice caught in his throat and Skye reached out to squeeze his hand.

'I wish I could have met her,' Skye said.

'She would have loved you,' Gethin said with a watery smile. 'You lost your dad?' he asked, his voice soft and kind.

Skye could feel her throat tighten and knew that she wouldn't be able to say the words and so simply nodded her head. Gethin squeezed her hand back.

'Sorry. I didn't mean to make you sad.'

Skye swallowed.

'You didn't,' she managed to say, feeling some of the weight shift. 'It's just that the memories are hard, you know?'

Gethin nodded.

'I see her everywhere. Sometimes I'm sure I can hear her voice. She loved this place but sometimes I think I have to get away because she is everywhere.'

'That's one of the hardest things,' Skye said. 'All that we had is gone so I don't have much to remind me of him.'

As she started to speak, she knew that she was going to lose any remains of control. Her whole body started to shake and the sobs would not be held back.

Gethin placed his mug on the hay bale beside him and pulled Skye back into his arms. He didn't say anything. He seemed to know there was nothing that could be said. Instead he held her close.

Skye could feel the pain start to subside. It always did, eventually, but this time she felt as if some of it had left her. She hadn't even told her friends in London what had happened. They knew she had lost her dad but nothing more. No-one had asked. Perhaps they sensed that she didn't want to talk about it.

It was unfair to compare them to Gethin. He, after all, had experienced the loss of his mum and so he understood. But she couldn't shake the feeling that he understood her, despite the obvious differences between them.

Skye eased herself out of his arms and this time Gethin seemed content to let her move, although he kept a hand on her arm. She looked up into his eyes and knew that was a mistake, if she wanted to get back to her life.

She looked away quickly, hoping that would break the spell, but it didn't. What was worse was when Gethin chuckled a little. Skye could feel her cheeks burn with indignation. Was he laughing at her?

She stood and took a few steps away before she turned to glare at him.

'What?' she demanded.

Gethin looked a little chastened, although whether that was because she had caught him in the act or because of what he was thinking, Skye wasn't sure.

'Sorry,' he said hurriedly, 'I was just thinking how parents know us better than we know ourselves, sometimes.'

Skye fixed him with her gaze but could detect no deceit or teasing. Although she wasn't sure what he meant by that, she decided the best thing was to let it go.

'We should be getting on,' Skye said in a way that told Gethin she was done with that particular conversation.

'I just want to check the injured leg. Give me a hand?' he said, his face returning to its serious expression as he walked over to the pen with the brightly bandaged sheep.

Skye pulled her gloves back on. She told herself it was to protect her injured hand, but really, she didn't want Gethin to see it.

She wasn't sure why. She knew that he would know she hadn't changed the bandage but it was more than that. Things had changed between them and the last thing her weak resolve needed right now was sympathy and caring.

Gethin showed her how to hold the sheep so he could inspect the bandage.

'Looks clean and dry. I'm going to leave it in place and we can check it tomorrow.'

Skye said nothing about the new use of the term 'we'. She couldn't allow herself to consider there could be a 'we'. There couldn't, unless she was prepared to give up everything she had worked for in London, her secure life.

And all that was nothing compared to the promise she had made herself, all those years before, that she would never live on a farm again in her life.

It was obvious that Gethin would never leave the land and so any possibility of a future was lost in that gulf between them. No, it would be better if they went back to the cool, distant relationship and simply worked together to get stuff done, then she could escape.

Gethin checked on the temporary wall, which seemed to have withstood the worst of the overnight weather. He nodded his approval at their efforts.

Skye led the way outside to the old tractor. She used the arm of her waterproof coat to sweep off the overnight snowfall.

Gethin walked around the tractor and then lifted the shovel out of the back and started to dig. His face crumpled a little as he walked and Skye suspected that his ankle was still painful.

She thought about offering to take over but suspected that Gethin wouldn't be keen to stand by and watch her do all the hard physical work.

Skye climbed into the cab and tried the key. The key turned but it was like a key in a child's toy. She wasn't rewarded with any noise or movement from the engine.

Gethin limped round and lifted the engine cover. His head disappeared for a few minutes but Skye was sure she knew the answer. It had seized in the bad weather which had probably caused more damage, and it would be unlikely that they could get it started again. They would have to go and see if the other tractor was driveable.

'I can't see anything obviously wrong. We're going to have to walk to the other tractor,' he said in a voice which suggested he wasn't relishing the idea.

'You could wait here and I'll go.'

Gethin shook his head.

'You won't be able to drive it back this way so I'll need to direct you to the farm.'

Skye nodded.

'What about your foot?'

She expected him to claim it was fine but instead he winced as he put weight on it.

'It's not great but I don't think we have much choice.'

Skye tried to hide her surprise at yet another change in his attitude and instead held out her arm.

Gethin hobbled over and threw one

arm around her shoulder. Skye put an arm around his waist and they moved off slowly, with Skye acting like a crutch.

They were both pink cheeked and a little puffed when they reached the tractor. It looked battered, exactly as if it had fallen sideways into a ditch. Gethin sucked in some air and this time Skye suspected the pain was all to do with the tractor and nothing to do with his ankle.

'Oh, Boris,' was all he said.

'Look, we know he'll start, so it's probably mostly cosmetic,' Skye said as they neared the tractor.

The door on the side that had fallen into the ditch was bent out of shape to such an extent that Skye was sure it would never open.

Gethin climbed in through the other side door and sat in the seat. He looked down at Skye and then turned the key. They both held their breath as nothing happened. Gethin turned his attention back to Boris, whacked the dashboard and turned the key and the tractor spluttered into life.

'My lady, your carriage awaits,' Gethin said before reaching out a hand to Skye.

She couldn't help it, she laughed, accepted the hand and stepped up into the cab beside him. She watched as Gethin winced as he pushed down the gas pedal.

'Let me?' Skye said, this time having no idea how he would react. Haughty and indignant or grateful? She once again felt like she was dealing with a different person, when he stood up on his good leg and moved so that she could sit in the driver's seat.

It was slow going and when they finally rumbled into the farmyard, Skye's head seemed to be throbbing in time to the beat of her heart, joining her hand in the same tattoo. She climbed down from the cab and had to blink hard several times to keep upright.

She reached out a hand for the side of the tractor, needing something solid to balance her out and winced as her injured hand gripped the tractor tight.

'Skye?' Gethin's voice was concerned and Skye was dimly aware that he was running to her side as she swayed.

Strong arms grabbed at her and prevented her from hitting the snow. Skye shook her head and some of the fogginess cleared.

'I'm fine,' she said but her voice sounded weak to her own ears and she knew she hadn't fooled Gethin.

'Of course you are,' he said as he swept her up in his arms and carried her into the house.

14

Painful Memories

Skye knew that she should insist on being put down. Her emotions were so confused, so tangled up together, that she could only think that closeness to Gethin, especially closeness like this, was only going to make that situation worse. He held her tight to his chest and once again she could hear his heart beating and it was a strange kind of comfort.

'What happened?' another voice said, which could only be Ren.

'I'm not sure. She was fine but then seemed to come over all dizzy.'

'Set her down here,' Ren said.

Skye realised that she was in their sitting-room as Gethin laid her gently on the shabby sofa.

A rough hand felt for her forehead.

'She has a fever.' Ren's voice again.

Another hand reached for Skye's bandaged hand and she tried to pull it away, feeling embarrassed and knowing that she was about to get a telling off.

She heard air sucked through teeth as Gethin pulled off her glove and inspected the bandage beneath.

'I'll get the kit,' Ren said and Skye could hear him make his way to the kitchen.

'You should have let me sort this, this morning,' Gethin said, but his voice sounded more worried than cross.

'I meant to do it myself but I forgot. I'm sure it's fine,' she added, even though she knew that it wasn't.

It hurt too much and she was aware that her whole body ached. She doubted it had anything to do with a night of sleeping on hay.

'You have a fever,' Gethin said and now he did sound cross, but Skye got the feeling that his anger wasn't aimed at her.

Gently, he unwrapped the bandage.

It was stuck in several places and Skye couldn't help but wince as he worked it loose.

'It's infected,' Gethin said, and Skye was pretty sure he was speaking to Ren, who had returned with the tin box.

'I'll get some hot water and antiseptic,' Ren said, disappearing once more.

Gethin pulled an old-fashioned mercury thermometer from the box, shook it a few times and then with a raised eyebrow placed it in Skye's mouth.

Gethin removed it and tutted as Ren returned with the bowl.

'Thirty-eight point four. Skye, I need to clean up the wound,' Gethin said before he picked up her hand and dipped it into the small bowl of hot water.

The water and antiseptic stung but Skye did her best not to let it show on her face. Once her hand had soaked for a while, Gethin peeled off the steristrips.

Gethin made short, expert work of drying the wound, covering it with a powder that once again sent a shot of pain up Skye's arm and then bandaging it with a clean and dry bandage.

'Are you allergic to any antibiotics?' he asked and Skye was more than a little taken with his bedside manner.

She shook her head as he dipped back into the box and brought out a small brown glass bottle. He shook out two red and yellow capsules and handed them to her with a glass of water. Once she had taken them, he proffered two more pills, which looked suspiciously like the painkillers that Ren claimed made him sleepy.

Skye didn't want to sleep. She had embarrassed herself by having a night-mare and now she was being all weak and feeble because her hand was a little infected.

She shook her head but one look at Gethin's expression and she knew that she didn't have the energy to argue, so with a sigh she held out her good hand and took the pills.

Gethin looked satisfied that she had

followed his instructions and leaned towards her. For a moment Skye thought that he was going to kiss her but instead he scooped her back up into his arms and carried her up the stairs to her room.

He dropped her gently on to the bed and kneeled down to pull off her boots.

Skye lay down and Gethin grabbed the blanket that was folded over the end of the bed and covered her with it.

Skye closed her eyes and so she wasn't sure if she was asleep and dreaming, when Gethin, or maybe it was the dreamworld Gethin, leaned down and kissed her on the forehead.

⋆ ⋆ ⋆

When she woke, Skye knew that she wasn't alone. She couldn't see anything, since the room was pitch dark, but she could sense that someone was there.

As she rolled on to her side, her injured hand made contact with the bed and all the memories came flooding back. She sat up suddenly and then wished she hadn't as her head seemed to swim and she felt as though someone had hit her on the back of the head.

'Steady,' a voice said, before reaching over and turning on the lamp that sat on the bedside table. Even the dim light from the lamp made Skye close her eyes and it was a few moments before she felt she could open them.

She felt the bed give and when she opened her eyes, Gethin was perched on the edge.

'How are you feeling?' he asked, his eyes studying her face. Skye didn't answer straightaway. It felt like her brain was on some kind of delay.

Gethin started to shake his hand and before Skye could make her mouth form words, she found herself pre-sented with the thermometer again.

'Temperature's down to thirty-eight but not back to normal yet.' He shook the thermometer down and then placed it carefully back into its case. 'Here, more antibiotics.'

Skye accepted the tablets and the glass of water. She took them and her brain was finally ready to tell her that she did feel better than earlier, which in truth wasn't saying much.

'Do you mind if I take a look at your hand?' Gethin said and Skye dutifully presented her hand as there was a gentle knock on the door.

'Can I come in?' It was Ren's voice.

'Of course,' Skye said, finding her own.

Ren came in carrying a tray of two steaming mugs and a plate of what looked and smelled like bacon sandwiches. Skye's stomach growled in happy response and Ren chuckled.

'I figured you'd be hungry. Good to see you looking better, lass. How are you feeling?'

'Better,' Skye said with a smile but what she couldn't ignore now was the nagging guilt that, once again, the two farmers had had to come to her rescue.

'Temperature's still up,' Gethin said

and Ren and Skye exchanged looks.

'In that case, you should eat up and get some more sleep,' Ren said and he disappeared back through the door.

'What time is it?' Skye asked.

'After ten,' Gethin said, handing her a mug of hot chocolate.

One sip told her that it had been made the old-fashioned way, with milk, just like her dad used to make it.

She took a sip and tried not to let the memories crowd in. She put the mug down on the bedside table and accepted a plate piled high with sandwiches. Gethin helped himself and they ate together in silence.

'I'm sorry,' Gethin said and Skye frowned.

'For what?'

'For dragging you out into the countryside and getting stranded. Your hand wouldn't have got infected if you had stayed here.'

Gethin was looking away from her and out the window, into the darkness beyond. Skye reached out a hand for his arm, to get his attention.

'It's my fault, Gethin. I'm perfectly capable of looking after myself.'

Gethin raised an eyebrow and then they both laughed, breaking some of the tension.

'OK, so normally I'm good at looking after myself. I'll admit that over the last few days I have required a fair amount of rescuing.'

'I don't mind,' Gethin said and he was smiling but there was something else in his expression, something that Skye couldn't pin down.

'Sometimes it seems like you do.' Skye said the words softly.

She didn't want to get into an argument, but whatever was happening with Gethin was confusing her emotions and she couldn't think straight, waiting for each time his mood would change.

'It's hard when you've lost someone close to you. It makes you afraid of . . . '

Skye nodded. This she did understand.

'It's hard to care when you know what pain might be waiting for you. Mum and Da were my world . . . '

Skye moved the plate off her lap and reached for his hand. Since she had told him at least part of her story, he knew that she understood.

'Da says I have a lot of bottled up anger.'

'I'd be hard pushed to disagree with him,' Skye said with a chuckle.

Gethin raked a hand through his hair, making it stand up at odd angles.

'It's not just Mum,' he said finally and this was what Skye had been waiting for him to share.

She had guessed as much from what she had overheard Ren saying.

'You don't have to tell me,' Skye said.

She wanted to know but she also knew how hard it was to repeat the past, how the words brought back the memories and then the inevitable pain.

Gethin looked at her and she didn't need to hear his words to know his pain. It was written all over his face.

15

Only a Heartbeat Away

'There was this girl . . . ' Gethin began. Skye squeezed his hand in what she hoped was an encouraging way but Gethin's eyes had travelled to a place in the past.

'I thought there might be,' Skye said softly, shifting her position so that she was sitting next to Gethin on the bed.

'We looked after Mum at home but when she got really sick we needed help.' Gethin's voice was hoarse with emotion and Skye could see that his eyes were full of tears.

'We had a team of nurses that would come out and help. One, her name was Caitlyn, used to come and sit with Mum at nights. I couldn't sleep so I would sit up with her too and so Caitlyn and I would talk.'

Gethin stood, walked to the window and looked out into the blackness.

'I thought that we had something. I was sure of it and it was the only thing that made life bearable, you know?'

He turned to look at Skye who nodded and tried to convey her understanding.

'No-one could ever replace Mum but Caitlyn understood that. I thought she understood me. After Mum . . . ' he couldn't seem to bring himself to say the words ' . . . well, she would pop in when she could, usually for breakfast, after her shift and we would talk.'

Gethin shook his head like he was trying to dislodge the memory.

'For a while there I thought I was in love, I know I was. Afterwards, everyone tried to tell me it was the grief, that I was reading things into a situation that weren't there.'

He turned back to the window and Skye could see that he had clenched both his fists.

'She didn't feel the same?' Skye asked and moved to stand beside him at the window.

There was nothing to see, the moon was hidden from sight by the thick cloud. All she could see was her reflection, standing next to Gethin and the anguish on his face.

'She said it was part of her role to support her patients through the transition period after bereavement and that all she had intended to do was her job. She said that a relationship between us could never work and that she was sorry if she had given me a false impression.'

'I'm sorry.'

The words sounded hollow, as if they didn't reflect the pain that Gethin must have felt back then, and what he clearly felt now.

'I was hurt and angry.'

'I'm guessing my arrival was a bit of a reminder?'

Gethin shook his head.

'I know I was rude and detached but

I just couldn't go there again, you know?'

'I do,' Skye said and returned to sit on the bed.

Despite the fact that she had slept for hours, she felt suddenly weary.

'My dad just gave up, after the farm. It was like he had nothing to live for. I wasn't enough . . . ' Skye swallowed.

Gethin crossed the room and sat by her.

'What about your mum?'

'She left when I was small. She remarried and has a new family. I see her occasionally but it's difficult.'

Gethin nodded.

'After my dad, I knew what I had to do,' Skye continued. 'I left Scotland, I left all of it and I created a whole new life.'

'In London?'

Skye nodded.

'I thought that the best way was to live somewhere that was completely different, to isolate myself, I guess, from all the things that could cause me pain.'

'Did it work?'

'For a while, I thought it did.'

'Then fate brought you here?' Gethin's tone was gruff, as if he was preparing himself for an answer that he didn't want to hear.

'To you.'

She knew she shouldn't say the words. She didn't know how she felt, not really. Her brain was warning her and everything that Gethin had told her should have urged caution, but her heart was having none of it.

'I'm glad you crashed your car in the snow,' Gethin whispered. 'I'm glad you chose the most unsuitable hire car for the conditions too.'

They both giggled.

'Well, it was the complete opposite of what I would have done in my past life.'

'But still it brought you here.'

'It did.'

Skye could feel all the unasked questions hanging in the air. Without warning, she yawned.

'You need to rest.'

Skye nodded but was reluctant to let him go. She wanted to ask him to stay, just to hold her until she fell asleep but was worried that she was being selfish. The last thing she wanted to do was hurt him. If he read more into that than she was sure of, she didn't think she could forgive herself.

'I could stay, if you like?' he asked shyly and Skye didn't trust herself to speak so she lay down and nodded. He stood and tucked her in, his eyes locked on hers and Skye felt sure in that moment that she had given away her heart.

Gethin went to sit in the chair but Skye reached out a hand for his. He stopped.

'Like last night?' she said, her voice quiet and uncertain.

He looked at her for a long while before he nodded. She shifted across the bed and he lay down beside her. Skye turned on her side and Gethin held out his arms and pulled her to him. Skye closed her eyes and listened to his heartbeat.

162

★ ★ ★

When Skye woke, she thought that they were back in the barn, that the day before had been a dream. She felt hemmed in on all sides by warm, furry lumps and she couldn't help but wonder how the sheep had escaped from their pens.

Opening her eyes, she could see that not only was she sharing the bed with Gethin, but they had also been joined by both of the sheepdogs. Bryn, who was nearest Skye, gave her face a lick.

'Bryn, mate, not everyone appreciates your kisses.' Gethin gently pushed the dog's face away.

'How are you feeling?'

Skye stretched and all the messages from her body were good.

'Much better.'

'Let me see your hand,' Gethin said and Skye pulled her hand from under the covers.

Lying on his back, Gethin gently unwrapped the bandage and seemed happy with what he saw.

'It's a lot less red but you'll need to take the antibiotics for a couple more days, at least.'

Skye nodded.

'Yes, Doctor.'

Gethin laughed.

'We keep a stock of supplies just in case we get cut off and I've done a first-aid course, but that's about it.'

'You have an excellent bedside manner,' she said as he reached for the first-aid tin and pulled out another bandage.

Gethin waggled his eyebrows and Skye giggled. The last few days had been such a rollercoaster but she had woken up feeling like the world was righting itself again.

'How's your foot?' Skye asked as Gethin finished bandaging.

Gethin lay back and lifted his leg in the air. Skye could see his ankle had shrunk back to near normal levels, and he could now wiggle his toes. He turned his head to Skye so that they were almost nose to nose. Skye held her breath as Gethin moved an inch closer . . .

Whatever he was going to do, he stopped as a loud crash sounded from downstairs. Gethin managed to frown and laugh at the same time.

'That's my dad's subtle way of telling me I'm late to start the rounds.'

'We can't have that,' Skye said, rolling out of bed on the other side.

She glanced at the window. For the first time in days, the sun was shining brightly and there were no snow clouds. She would probably be able to get back to her hire car and then head out to the manor.

The problem was, and she could hardly believe it herself, she didn't really want to.

Gethin went ahead of her down the stairs but he held a hand out behind him, and she took it, letting him lead her down to the ground floor. Gethin stopped on the last step and Skye nearly walked into him.

'What is it?' she asked as she peeked over his shoulder and out of the front door, which was standing ajar.

16

A Fish Out of Water

All Skye could do was blink in surprise. Parked in front of the farmhouse was a top of the range off-road vehicle, complete with snow chains. It was a dazzling black against the white backdrop.

A man in designer wellingtons walked around the side of the black car, with Ren trying to keep up. The man raised a hand and waved it in her direction.

'Who's that?' Skye said, turning to Gethin, intending to grin at the over-the-top country manner of the man, who couldn't have looked more out of place if he'd tried.

The smile died on her lips when she saw Gethin's face ruined by the scowl that she had thought she would never see again.

'That's your Lord of the Manor,' Gethin said. His voice had lost its playfulness.

Skye went to open her mouth to say something in her defence but closed it again. It was clear from the look on his face that he wasn't going to find any humour in the situation, however ridiculously dressed the man was.

Skye sighed and stepped off the stairs, conscious of her appearance. This was not the impression that she had hoped to make. For one thing, other than her jeans she was wearing borrowed, old clothes. She knew she had hay in her hair and she hadn't yet cleaned her teeth.

She winced, then plastered a smile on her face before walking confidently across the farmyard with her hand outstretched.

'Mr Raleigh? It's a pleasure to finally meet you.'

Skye found her hand firmly shaken and tried not let the wince show as she could feel the steri-strips on her hand pull.

'Miss Mackenzie!' he said, sounding delighted but Skye suspected that was how he always sounded. 'I thought I would pop along and rescue you.'

Skye stared wide-eyed for a split second and flashed Ren an apologetic expression, hoping to convey that was not how she felt at all.

'I've been well looked after by Ren and Gethin, I can assure you,' Skye said, trying to keep her voice light.

'I'm sure you have,' Raleigh said looking her up and down, taking in her dishevelled appearance and the fact that she had been clearly out working. 'Well, if you are happy to let me steal her away?'

He turned to address these words to Ren and Skye closed her eyes briefly and wished she were anywhere but here.

'Skye is free to do as she pleases. She has kindly helped us out, which we are mighty grateful for.' Ren turned and smiled at Skye and she knew that she, at least, was forgiven.

Skye crossed the small space between them and threw her arms around his neck.

'Thank you for everything, Ren. I'm sorry about . . . ' Her voice trailed off. She didn't know how to explain what had just happened.

'No need for you to apologise, lass, and we do appreciate all your help.'

'I just need to go and get my belongings,' Skye said, turning to Raleigh, who waved the comment away.

'I'll send a man back to collect them,' he said, as if they were unimportant, or perhaps he just didn't want to spend any more time than strictly necessary in the presence of farmers.

'I'll come back for them later,' Skye said firmly, turning to Ren. 'I promise.'

Skye knew she had to come back, to say thank you and to apologise properly. She couldn't leave it like this.

Gethin was standing in the farm-house doorway, looking on.

'Thanks for all your help, Gethin,' she called, even though it was no use.

Gethin had turned away. It was clear that he was pointedly ignoring her and she had the distinct feeling that she had just crossed an invisible line and without realising it, joined the other side.

'If you've said your goodbyes, I would like to get going?' Raleigh said.

Skye tried to smile. This was good. She needed to go and do her job and the fact that he had come to collect her suggested that he was keen to hear her pitch, too, but to leave things as they were was awkward.

'I'll be back,' she whispered to Ren before pulling the door of the sleek car open and climbing in. She had barely shut the door, when Raleigh put his foot down and sped out of the farmyard.

Skye risked a glimpse in the side mirror. There was no sign of Gethin but Ren stood there and watched her go, raising a hand in goodbye before turning away and heading indoors.

'I had no idea they would put you to work. Absolutely shocking. I know the locals have their own way of doing things but really . . . ' Raleigh sounded outraged.

'I offered to help, Mr Raleigh.'

Skye didn't want to bring up her past but she couldn't just sit there and let him bad mouth Ren and Gethin without coming to their defence.

'I grew up on a farm so I'm used to it.'

Raleigh threw her a glance, with an eyebrow raised in surprise.

'I thought you were based in London.'

'I am, but before that I lived with my dad on a farm in Scotland.'

Skye hoped that would be the end of it and when Raleigh appeared lost in thought, she decided to move the conversation on.

'I have some ideas about the castle that I think you are going to like, to maximise its earning potential.'

'In the early stages I feel getting the right people is the most important objective,' Raleigh said and Skye was sure that Ren and Gethin would never qualify as the 'right' people.

★　★　★

Skye was standing in the large bay window of the castle's modern extension. This was the part of the building where Raleigh and his family lived. It was all smooth lines and sleek furniture and Skye personally thought it was out of step with both the surroundings and the restored castle next door.

She was dressed in a fresh pair of jeans and a blouse which had been offered to her by the hostess. Mrs Raleigh looked as if she would have preferred that Skye strip off on the doorstep rather than walk in wearing her stained and sheep-smelling clothes. Not that the Lady of the Manor would ever be responsible for clearing up any mess.

Skye couldn't help wondering what she would have made of the place had she travelled here directly without the diversion to the farm. Before, she was sure she would have been suitably impressed by the beautifully manicured lawns and gardens, not to mention the buildings which had been interior designed to within an inch of their lives.

But now it felt fake, false somehow.

She had adored the countryside around her home, it felt part of her and she had felt a familiar sensation at the farm, despite the fact that the landscape was completely different. But being here, now, she felt like a fish out of water.

An image of Gethin, studiously ignoring her then turning away, crossed her mind. Not that she could blame him. Everything that she had heard so far of Raleigh's business plans, told her that he knew nothing about the local culture of farming and worse than that, he didn't seem to care. It wasn't Skye's place to point this out, her boss would be horrified that she was even thinking those thoughts, but she couldn't help it.

There was a way to make the castle and manor successful, and keep the locals on side, but she doubted that Raleigh would listen and if he did, it would most likely result in her being fired.

'Amazing view,' Raleigh said as an older woman bustled into the room with a tray of coffee and home-made cakes. He nodded to the woman, although whether it was a thank you or a dismissive nod, Skye wasn't sure and none of it was making her feel more comfortable.

'I have to admit I was surprised by your presentation,' he said as he folded himself into one of the ultra-modern leather chairs.

Skye forced herself to focus. She was going to be heading back to London in a few days, back to the life she had worked so hard for. Was she really prepared to throw that all away? All she needed to do was her job, advise on promotion of the business and offer the company's event management team's service.

It wasn't her place to tell this man what he should do with his business. It wasn't as if anything he had suggested was illegal.

Skye took a deep breath and smiled, before taking a seat and accepting a cup of strong, Italian filter coffee.

'We can offer you what you want and need, with the advantage that you only have to deal with one company for both PR and event management. I can show you some of the mock-ups we have designed, once I have retrieved my luggage.'

Raleigh studied her thoughtfully.

'There is no need for you to go back. I have people who can collect your things.'

'I appreciate that,' Skye said firmly, 'but Ren and his son were very kind to me and I would like to go back and thank them properly.'

For a moment Skye thought he was

going to argue as he studied her.

'We have no formal agreement as yet, but I hope I can be assured of your loyalty.'

Skye blinked, not sure what she was being accused of or why.

'Of course,' she finally said.

'Then you may go, but please do not discuss any business matters with your new friends.' He said the words as if they were offensive to him.

Skye nodded. She had no idea why Raleigh was so concerned about her sharing confidential information with Ren and Gethin. She doubted they would have the smallest bit of interest in what was going on up at The Manor and castle.

17

Disturbing Discovery

Skye was waiting for her lift back to the farm. She had been told that someone would be with her in the next ten minutes. In the meantime, she was exploring the perfectly tended gardens that surrounded the new build that was known as The Manor. The gardens were so neat and tidy that Skye felt her very presence was somehow a blot on the landscape.

As she walked, she thought about the response she would get when she returned to her office in London. She was sure that she had won over Raleigh. That would mean a very lucrative contract for the business and Skye wouldn't be surprised if it meant a promotion for her. It was possible that she might get to oversee the contract, too, which sent a fizz of excitement through her.

'Do you think it wise to let her go back to those people. What if she tells them?'

Skye recognised the clipped tones of Mrs Raleigh, who had not bothered to hide her mystification at Skye's apparent loyalty to her rescuers.

Mrs Raleigh had not been won over by Skye and that was something she would need to work on.

Although, once she retrieved her luggage, Skye would be able to dress in a way that no doubt Mrs Raleigh would be more comfortable with.

'I haven't spoken about that part of my plan, I'm not a complete idiot, my darling.'

Skye knew she shouldn't be listening, knew that she should walk quickly away. But her legs refused to obey her.

She closed her eyes, willing Raleigh to say something that would have no impact on Gethin and his dad. Something she, and her conscience, could ignore.

'The castle needs a moat, darling. Without it, it's just, well, a building.'

Skye frowned. She was sure Gethin wouldn't care two hoots whether the castle had a moat or not. Why did it matter if she heard them speak about that?

'Restoring the moat will mean diverting the river, my love,' Raleigh said in a heavy tone, as if he were trying to explain a complicated principle to someone who was being particularly dim. 'We have the right to do it but it won't make us very popular with the public.'

'What difference does it make to them, anyway? They complain whenever we change anything. Honestly, you would think they would be grateful.'

Skye could hear Mrs Raleigh pace up and down, her high heels clipping on the wooden floor.

'I doubt they will be grateful that their principle water source is now flowing into a ditch around the castle.' Mr Raleigh didn't bother to hide the sarcasm from his voice, at his wife's lack of understanding.

'Why can't they just turn on a tap, like everyone else? Surely they have running water in those hovels they call home?'

Skye felt frozen to the spot but knew she needed to move. She couldn't risk being seen. If they knew she had overheard them speaking, she had no idea what that would mean for the contract.

Finally, her legs started to move and she scurried away with her head ducked down. Once she was back at the front of The Manor, she tried to calm her heart, which was pounding loudly in her chest.

How had this happened? This should have been the best day of her professional life but she could feel something cold and heavy in the pit of her stomach and she knew that sensation wouldn't go away.

Another sleek off-road vehicle drew up in front of her. This one was a dark maroon and had the family crest of the Raleighs printed on the side in gold leaf.

The driver climbed out, walked round and opened the door for her. Skye climbed in, giving him a small smile of thanks. All she could think about were the words she had over-heard and what that would mean to Gethin and Ren, not to mention the other farmers.

There had been newcomers to Scotland when Skye's family had farmed there. Most had been sensitive to the land and the natural flow of things but a few had not and their impact had been vast.

Raleigh clearly had no such sensitiv-ity and the fact that he was hiding his plans from the surrounding landowners only made him sound more guilty.

Skye rested her head back and closed her eyes. This should have been a straightforward deal, one that she could take back to the London office and silence those that had thought she wasn't up to the task. She wasn't supposed to be faced with a dilemma where her allegiances were tested, as were her morals.

She had an informal contract with Raleigh, which would have consequences if she broke, but could she keep what she knew from Gethin and Ren? They would find out eventually, of course, but most likely when the river dried up.

For a moment Skye almost asked the driver to let her out and to go to the farm without her to collect her luggage. If she didn't see them again, perhaps she could keep her secret?

Skye's dad appeared in her mind's eye. He didn't say anything — he didn't have to. Skye knew that she couldn't just ignore the consequences. If she did, they would eat away at her. She knew that her father would have been disappointed with her and that was something she didn't think she could ignore.

The driver made his way down the

lane that led to the farm. The roads near to the manor and castle had been cleared, with what Skye suspected was a snow plough of sorts, so they had made quick progress but now they had slowed to a crawl as the driver had to navigate the compacted snow and snow drifts.

His look of concentration also seemed to hold some condemnation, as if he was annoyed at having to risk the SUV's paintwork on a mission such as this.

The driver stopped the car at the entrance to the farmyard.

'I'll wait here for you, miss.'

Skye nodded and climbed out. It would mean she had to carry her suitcase across the farmyard but right now she didn't care.

As she walked across the yard, she noticed that Gethin had obviously cleared some of the snow as there was a clear path to the various outbuildings.

The front door opened and a black, white and tan blur rushed towards her.

'Hey, Bryn,' she said.

She didn't feel like smiling with the dilemma she faced but somehow, she couldn't help it. Bryn, at least was pleased to see her.

Skye leaned down and stroked his head and Bryn leaned in to her. She could feel him nudge her leg and laughed when she realised that he was trying to herd her towards the front door and no doubt, the warmth of the kitchen.

'OK, I get the message,' she said as she started to walk again, with Bryn close at her heels.

Ren's face appeared at the kitchen window and he waved for her to come in. Skye couldn't ignore the fact that she felt more at home here than she did at The Manor.

She shook her head to try and dislodge the thought. Of course she did. This was familiar but only because of her past — what she needed to think about now was the future. The only problem with that was the past wasn't content to stay silent.

It was possible that the new moat would have no effect on Gethin and Ren, but somehow, she doubted it. The real question was whether she could keep quiet, whether she could look them in the eye.

'Hello, lass!' Ren greeted her warmly as she stepped into the kitchen.

He opened his arms for a hug and Skye stepped into them, fighting against the memories of coming home to her dad at their farm.

'I hope the Lord of the Manor treated you right.'

He said the words with a smile and there was no trace of any malice. Ren was a live and let live kind of man.

'It's all about a high standard of living up there, Da. You know that.'

The same could not be said of Gethin, whose voice dripped with sarcasm and disgust.

'How did it feel to dine with the enemy?' Gethin's face was set hard and there was no trace of the side of him that Skye had seen before.

She couldn't work out if that was going to make this whole thing easier or worse.

18

A Terrible Dilemma

Skye didn't think it was worth speaking to Gethin about how she had felt slightly out of place and certainly inappropriately dressed up at the manor, or the fact that she felt more at home here. The last thing she wanted to do was get into an argument.

'Hush, son,' Ren said and gave Gethin a warning look.

Gethin stared into his mug of tea and looked like he was going to pretend that she wasn't there.

Ren handed Skye a mug of tea and she took it gratefully. The driver was going to have to wait in the car but then it had top of the range heating so no doubt he wouldn't complain at the delay.

'I've heard the place is looking mighty fine.'

Gethin snorted but Skye ignored him and kept her focus on Ren.

'They've certainly done a lot of work but to me it looks a little overdone, if you know what I mean?'

Ren nodded and gave her a smile. She smiled back.

'Looks like I might have won the contract though,' she added.

It was exciting to say the words out loud but the fact that they were followed by a stab of guilt, took the shine off it a bit.

'That's wonderful. Congratulations!' Ren sounded genuinely pleased and that was difficult to hear.

Skye tried to convince herself that the changes to The Manor and the castle would only be good for Ren and Gethin. She had suggested that Raleigh use local products from local farmers and that could be a selling point. Raleigh had at least said he would consider the idea.

'Thanks. I think it'll be good for you too. I've persuaded Mr Raleigh to stock local produce, so it should raise your profile.'

Ren smiled and nodded but Skye had the distinct feeling that was for her benefit only and wondered if Ren could read her mind.

Gethin stood up.

'Where are you going?' Ren asked, somewhat sharply.

'Work,' Gethin said shortly.

'The weather's going to close in again, so you'll have to take me with you.' Ren took one last gulp of his tea and then stood up, but took much of his weight through his arms on the table.

'Da, your knee's the size of a rugby ball. Sit yourself down. I can manage.'

Ren was shaking his head.

'You won't get it done in time. I don't want you stuck in the top barn again.'

Ren tried to take a step, but his knee had other ideas and seemed to fold beneath him. Skye managed to reach for him just in time to prevent him crashing to the floor.

Once he was steady again, she guided him back to the bench.

'I'll help,' Skye said. 'I'll ask the driver to come back for me in a few hours.'

'I doubt the weather will hold long enough, lass,' Ren said.

'Then I'll ask him to come back for me in the morning. I can finish my business with Mr Raleigh and head off back to London.'

Gethin's eyes were fixed on his dad and Skye could tell he was torn.

He clearly didn't want her help but then he didn't want his dad to insist on sharing the workload either. There was a look of resignation and it seemed clear that Skye had won.

'Great,' Skye said before there were any arguments. 'I'll let the driver know and meet you out front.'

Skye walked purposefully out of the kitchen without looking at Gethin's face. She could do this. She would help them out one last time and hopefully that would salve her conscience and then she could return her focus to the career-making contract that she was sure she was going to get signed.

★   ★   ★

They travelled in silence. Gethin was still limping but had climbed into the driver's seat in such a way that Skye knew it was pointless to argue with him. If he wanted to drive on a painful foot then she was going to let him. She didn't think she had room in her brain for an argument with him.

They rolled up behind the old tractor that sat exactly where they had left it.

Gethin climbed down and walked to the small door in the side of the barn, opened it and went in. Skye followed in his wake, wishing once again that this whole thing was over and she could return to her neat, uncomplicated life in London.

'We need to clear out each pen,' Gethin said and it was clearly hard work for him to speak to her but he seemed to know they couldn't get the work done unless he did.

He opened a gate in one pen and walking behind the ten sheep in the pen, moved them into the next empty one. He then turned and opened the large double doors at the far end of the barn, coming back with a wheelbarrow.

'If I load up the wheelbarrow, can you chuck the hay on the pile out the back?' His manner seemed to have softened a little and Skye suspected that he didn't think his ankle was up to the trundling back and forth.

'Of course,' Skye said and as soon as Gethin had loaded up the first wheel-barrow load she did as she had been directed.

Once the floor of the pen was clear of straw, Gethin went back outside and returned with a bucket.

He threw the contents on the floor and then used a brush to clean the concrete floor. There was a small channel that ran the full length of the barn that took the dirty water away.

'Where do you get the water from?' Skye asked before she could think about how wise it was to voice that question. Surely Gethin would be suspicious.

'Water comes from the river,' Gethin said, grunting with the effort.

Skye swallowed the lump that appeared in her throat. Where did she think the water came from? She was brought up on a farm and knew better than Mrs Raleigh. You didn't run water mains out to isolated farm buildings like this.

'You went down to the river?' Skye asked, distracted by her own thoughts.

Gethin stopped brushing and leaned on his broom, resting his injured foot on his good foot, taking the weight off of it.

'No, my grandfather built a series of clay pipes that divert some of the water from the river into a water trough.'

Gethin was studying her face and Skye was worried that she would give something away, so she turned and pretended to busy herself moving the wheelbarrow into position for the next pen.

'Do we need to check on the injured sheep?' Skye said, reaching for any subject that would steer the conversation in a different direction while she tried to work out if she could keep what she knew to herself.

'We'll need to change the bandage,' Gethin said but Skye could still feel his eyes on her.

She had no choice but to turn her attention back to him, or appear rude. She felt his eyes studying her face and she tried to keep her expression blank but she knew she couldn't do this.

She didn't want to break her confidence or her contract but she knew that if she didn't at least warn Gethin and Ren guilt would eat her up.

Skye nodded as Gethin took a step towards her.

'What's wrong?' he asked and this time it was as though she was back with the Gethin from their night stranded in the barn — the Gethin that understood her and made her feel like she was home, for the first time in a long time.

Skye bit her lip. She didn't want to cry but the unfairness of the situation that she found herself in was almost too much. Whichever decision she made would have consequences.

Gethin had crossed the distance between them and was now standing so that she would be able to reach out and touch him. Skye shook her head, more at herself than anything else.

She had no idea what to do. If she told Gethin, she would be fired, she knew that and most likely her reputation would be ruined and she would never get another job in London, but she also knew she couldn't live with the secret.

She knew the pain of losing land — land that was part of you — in a way that many didn't understand.

Her eyes pricked and she knew that she was crying, but before she could say anything, she found herself pulled into Gethin's arms, the one place where she felt safe and like she belonged, however much she fought against the idea.

'Whatever it is, you can tell me,' Gethin whispered into her hair but all Skye could do was shake her head.

'You'll hate me.' Her voice shook on each word and she could barely get the words out.

'I could never hate you,' he said slowly and tightened his grip around her.

That only made Skye feel worse. He should hate her! She had actually thought about not telling him what she knew.

Leaving him, no doubt, to find out when it would be too late and the consequences for the farm that he loved would be too great, possibly the end of it.

'You will when I tell you.'

'Do you trust me?' he asked and Skye closed her eyes and listened to his heart beat in his chest.

Skye had schooled herself not to rely on anyone else, not after her mum, not after losing the farm. She had needed to be independent and self-sufficient.

It might not be the secret to a happy life but it certainly reduced the risk of pain and loss.

'Yes.'

She said the words before she realised what she was saying. She analysed the word and found that, deep down, it was the truth.

Gethin released his tight grip but kept one arm around her shoulders and moved her so that they could sit side by side on the hay bale.

'I know that I've been a bit all at sea with my attitude,' he said and he was clearly a little embarrassed.

'You could say that,' Skye said and Gethin laughed. It was a warm, comforting sound and to Skye's ears sounded genuine.

'I've been hurt before and I guess my self-protection mechanism is a little over developed.'

'Funny, I think I have one of those, too.'

They sat in companionable silence for a few moments and Skye leaned into Gethin, who rested his chin on Skye's head.

'The thing is . . . ' she started to say as the words seemed to catch in her throat, 'I think you might have been right about me.'

The words came out so fast that they seemed to bleed into one another.

19

Words of Love

'Now, that I don't believe,' Gethin said and he brushed hair from Skye's tear-stained cheek.

'You said it yourself. I dined with the enemy.'

Skye felt rather than heard Gethin sigh.

'I was being childish, Skye. You have a job to do and I respect that. I just don't particularly like Raleigh.'

Skye smiled, thinking that was an understatement.

'OK, I'm not keen on city folk who don't understand the land, coming and taking over, but you might be right. This could be good for us.'

Skye shifted so that she could see Gethin's face.

'But he is the enemy.' She knew what

she was going to do now and she couldn't believe that she had ever thought she would do anything different. She couldn't keep this from Gethin and Ren. She couldn't risk the farm.

Losing the farm had driven her dad to an early grave and there was no way she could stand around and let that happen to someone else, not if she had any power at all to do something about it.

'Skye,' Gethin's voice held a warning note, 'if you have information about Raleigh's business . . . '

'I know, I know,' Skye said, cutting through his words.

She didn't want him to have to say them to her, as if she didn't know what she needed to do.

'I need to tell you.'

Gethin's expression wasn't what she was expecting. He looked slightly shocked.

'The opposite, actually.'

Skye stared.

'But . . . '

'The information is confidential, right?'

Skye nodded.

'And you wouldn't have access to this information unless you were directly involved, as part of your job.'

Skye nodded again. If her emotions had been at war before, now she felt completely overwhelmed. Gethin wasn't saying any of the things she had expected.

'If you told me, there would be consequences?' Gethin asked. Again, his tone was gentle, so full of understanding that Skye could feel the tears start to flow.

'I'd lose my job and maybe get sued.'

'Then you can't tell me,' Gethin said as if it was the most obvious thing in the world.

'If you hadn't crashed your car into the snowdrift we wouldn't need to have this conversation.'

'But there will be consequences for you and your dad.'

'They were always going to happen,

whether you knew about them or not,' Gethin said.

Skye shook her head. She had been worried that he would be angry with her, furious even, but this was much worse.

'I can't keep this a secret.'

'I'm not sure you have much choice,' Gethin said.

He looked down at her and smiled, but Skye wasn't fooled. She could see the worry written all over his face.

'You don't understand. I can't keep this a secret. I won't be able to live with myself. It's like history repeating itself.'

They sat in silence and Skye was sure Gethin was trying to work out the connection.

'We lost our farm, Gethin. We lost everything. It had been in my dad's family for generations and then one day it was gone. The land was part of my dad, you know? It killed him to leave it. He was never the same, like he had given up on life and then one day he was gone, too.'

The force of the emotion was making her shiver and she turned and buried her face into Gethin's chest. He shifted so that he could lift her on to his lap and cradle her like a baby.

He didn't say anything, he didn't need to. Skye knew that he understood.

Unless you had land that was part of your history, part of your blood, a person couldn't truly understand. Gethin kissed her gently on the top of the head and rubbed her back. Skye felt that the wall she had built up, to keep the loss at bay, had finally broken down and the falling tears were taking some of the pain with them.

Skye wasn't sure how long she had been in Gethin's arms. It felt like for ever, but at the same time as though it could never be long enough. Gethin didn't seem to be worried about the time, either, just content to hold her as her sobs finally subsided.

'I can't ask you to risk your future,' Gethin said, 'however much I might want to.'

'I know the farm is important to you, more than that.'

Gethin chuckled.

'That's not what I meant.'

Skye shifted her head so that she could look up into his face. Seeing him smiling down at her, his own eyes soft, was almost more than her heart could take.

'I don't want to see you hurt in any way, Skye.'

'You losing the farm would hurt way more than losing my job,' Skye said in response.

She surprised herself more than Gethin, as she knew that the sentiment was true.

'But you've worked so hard to get where you are. I don't want you to throw all that away.'

'If I keep what I know to myself, I would lose a part of me anyway.'

Gethin's expression was questioning and Skye sighed, trying to work out how to explain it to him.

'I wouldn't be able to look at myself

in the mirror. It wouldn't be me. I just don't think I can live with knowing that I could have done something to help you.'

Gethin was studying her and Skye was untroubled by his gaze.

'I love you.'

Now it was his turn to blurt out the words and he looked shocked that he had said them out loud. He shook his head.

'Now I sound like I'm trying to manipulate your emotions to get what I want . . . '

Skye cut him off with a kiss. She lifted her lips to his and kissed him, gently. She had been fighting her feelings, but a part of her had known at that first meeting, despite how unpromising it had been. Gethin was a man that she understood, that she felt she knew, even though they had only known each other a few days.

Despite her best intentions she had lost her heart to him and she knew that whatever the complications or difficulties that would always be true.

Gethin broke the kiss first.

'I meant what I said,' he whispered before leaning in and kissing her again. 'I love you, Skye. I know it might sound crazy but I do.'

'No more crazy than me loving you,' Skye said, her voice low as if she was worried that someone would overhear her.

Skye didn't want to break the spell but she knew that this magical moment couldn't last, however much they might want it to. The real world would be banging on the door soon enough and they needed to talk about what that might mean.

'But . . . '

Gethin silenced her with a kiss.

'That can wait,' he murmured as he kissed her again.

Skye shook her head and he stopped, reluctantly.

'Your job?' he asked.

'What I know,' Skye said.

Her job was important, as was her life in London but it all seemed far away. She didn't think she could put any of that before Gethin and Ren.

It didn't matter if nothing came of her relationship with Gethin, she knew she couldn't stand by and let the worst happen to them, as it had to her family.

'You need to think about it,' Gethin said and placed a finger gently on her lips when she started to protest. 'Da and I will cope, we always have. This farm has seen tough times before and we'll get through it. I love you, Skye, and I only want what's best for you . . . ' He tilted his head to one side and stroked her cheek. 'Even if that's not me.'

Skye knew that she felt the same and wondered if this was what true love was — putting the needs of the one you love before your own.

'What's best for me, is not having to live with guilt for the rest of my life. I was raised to do the right thing, Gethin. One of the many lessons my dad taught me was that anyone can do the right thing when it's easy, when there aren't consequences.

'The real test of a person's character is doing the right thing even when it costs you.'

Gethin rocked her a little in his arms and she turned her face into his shirt, feeling like she wanted to fix this in her memory, in case it was the last time Gethin held her.

'I've been running away from the past, from the pain, but now I realise that I've been losing the person I was. The person my dad raised me to be. I wanted to get away from the pain so badly that I've created a life for myself that I thought would be safe.'

'Your dad sounds like he was an amazing man,' Gethin said, 'but then, that's farmers for you.'

They both laughed and, mixed together, it was a nice sound.

'I like to hear you laugh.'

'Me, too. We should probably try to do that more often.'

'What are we going to do?' Skye asked, not sure that she was actually asking Gethin, more the universe.

'Well, we are going to finish clearing out the pens and feed the sheep. Farm comes first after all.'

Skye smiled. Her dad used to say something similar.

'Then we are going to head back to the farmhouse and talk to my da. He's the wisest man I know. He'll know what to do.'

20

The Right Decision

Gethin, Ren and Skye were sitting around the long, worn kitchen table. Ren had insisted that they eat first and then talk, claiming that no good decisions were ever made on an empty stomach. When they all had eaten their fill, including a fruit crumble and custard, and were sipping at their coffee, Ren gave the signal that now they could talk.

'Right, then,' he said. 'Now, Skye, I'm guessing you heard something at the old castle that's troubling you and you want to share what you know with us.'

Skye stared at Ren, her mouth hanging open. Gethin just chuckled and smiled at his dad.

'Told you,' Gethin said to Skye.

She shook her head in astonishment

as Ren smiled at her.

'I may just be a farmer but I've been around for long enough to figure certain things out,' he said.

Skye reached out to squeeze his arm.

'There's no such thing as being 'just a farmer'.'

Ren nodded in appreciation but said nothing.

'Well . . . ' Skye started but Gethin flashed her a warning look.

'Da, if Skye shares what she knows she will lose her job and maybe worse.'

Ren nodded sagely.

'And let me guess. Skye, you want to tell us and Gethin here is worried for you.'

Ren didn't bother to try and keep the smile from his face.

Gethin sighed in an exaggerated manner.

'Yes, yes, Da. You're right.'

Skye looked from Gethin to Ren and back again.

'I like Skye — no, more than that — I love her, which is why I can't let her do this, not even for the sake of the farm.'

'Seems to me that Skye is the one that needs to make that decision,' Ren said, looking at Skye, who nodded. 'But before you do, Skye, you should know that whatever you decide is fine by us.'

'It's not fine by me.'

She looked into Ren's eyes and saw understanding there.

'I have to be able to look at myself in the mirror and I know I won't be able to if I don't tell you. Being here with you has reminded me who I am, who my father raised me to be.'

Gethin opened his mouth to speak but Skye turned to him and asked him to be silent with her eyes.

They gazed at each for a few moments and then Gethin reluctantly nodded his head.

He clasped his hands together on the table in front of him and Skye took that as a sign that she should continue.

'What Raleigh is planning to do is plain wrong, even if legally he has the right to do so. And to keep it a secret is beyond wrong, to give you no chance to fight it!'

Skye could feel the emotion catch in her throat and she had to stop speaking.

Gethin moved down the bench and threw an arm around her shoulder.

Skye leaned in to him, finding comfort from his nearness.

She took a few deep breaths and then sat up straight, absolutely sure now about what she needed to do.

'He's going to divert the river to reinstate the castle moat.'

There was an overwhelming sense of relief at having said the words out loud, followed closely by a sense that she had taken a hammer to her old life.

But whatever she was feeling was better than she had felt before she told them.

Skye looked up then, wondering at the silence. She could tell that the news was as bad as she feared.

'I'm so sorry' was all she could think of to say.

That seemed to break the spell and

Ren turned his attention to her and smiled.

'You have nothing to be sorry for, lass. I suspected it might be something like this, though I'm surprised he thinks he can do this without the proper authority.'

'He's probably paid some men off,' Gethin said grimly.

'I'm more surprised that he told you,' Ren said, directing his comment in Skye's direction.

She looked down at the table, studying its worn, pock-marked surface.

'He didn't exactly. I was waiting outside for the driver to bring me over here and I heard Raleigh and his wife discussing it.'

Skye jumped as Ren's booming laughter echoed around the kitchen.

'He may be rich but he certainly isn't wise.'

'What will you do now?' Gethin asked.

Skye shrugged. She had been trying to work out what she would do, but so far had come up with nothing.

It was probably best to quit before she got fired, then she might have some hope of getting another job.

'They've no way of knowing it was you who told us,' Gethin said hopefully but his expression changed when he saw Ren and Skye's reaction.

'Even if he doesn't guess, which I'm sure he will, I can't manage the contract. I can't be part of something that is so against what I believe to be right. I'm probably better off quitting before I get fired.'

'You will always have a place here, if you need some time to work things out.'

Skye said nothing. She had thought he might say something like that, part of her had even hoped that he would.

The thought made her heart swell but there was still that part of her that wasn't sure whether she could walk away from her life in London and come back to the land. The very thing that she had been running from.

Unbidden memories of her dad resurfaced and she was worried that she was going to break down.

'I think I might go to bed, if that's all right? It's been a long day.'

'Aye, lass. Off you go,' Ren said before Gethin could say anything more.

Skye walked out of the kitchen and could feel Gethin's eyes follow her.

She was torn between wanting to be with him, to sit up with him all night and talk it through, but she knew that she needed to figure this out herself and that Gethin would be a distraction that would sway her thoughts.

★   ★   ★

Skye had been awake until the early hours and so when she woke, it was later than she intended. She threw on some clothes and padded down the stairs. She had been unable to reach any conclusion about what she should do next. Her heart was clear, she wanted to be with Gethin and to be in a

217

place where she felt she belonged, but she couldn't shake the fear and loss that came with memories of her own past.

In the kitchen, Gethin and Ren looked as though they had already been out working and had returned for a late morning coffee.

'Did you get hold of him, Da?' Gethin said as Skye walked in.

'I did,' Ren said, smiling up at Skye.

'There's coffee in the pot, pet. I'd get up but . . . '

He didn't need to say any more as Skye crossed the kitchen and filled up a mug, before returning to the table and sitting down opposite Gethin. The look on his face when she sat down made her heart skip a beat and for a brief second her mind was made up.

'He's going to let the Farmers' Union know and get a meeting sorted as soon as they can. The weather seems to be on the change so it should be easier to organise.'

Skye felt the relief wash over her at the decision she had made. She had known it was the right thing to do, whatever the consequences. At least the local farmers now had a chance of changing the future.

'You must be starving. I'll make you some breakfast,' Gethin said, leaping up just as there was the sound of heavy hammering on the front door.

'Miss Mackenzie! I want to speak to you right now!'

Skye exchanged looks with both Gethin and Ren. There was no mistaking the tone or the voice.

'Sounds like the Farmers' Union have been at work,' Ren said. 'I'll go get the door.'

He lifted himself gently from his seat and then hobbled to the door.

Gethin stopped what he was doing and went to stand behind Skye, resting a reassuring hand on her shoulder.

'I'll be right here with you,' he said.

Skye placed her hand over his and braced herself for what was coming next.

21

Fear for the Future

'Who the devil do you think you are?' Raleigh rushed into the kitchen, leaving Ren in his wake. Raleigh's face was flushed with indignation and he seemed to have lost a little of his cut-glass accent.

'If you'll be so kind as to keep your voice at a civil level,' Ren said mildly as he took his seat back at the table.

Raleigh glared at him, as if he couldn't believe he was being lectured about manners by a man who worked the land.

'Perhaps you would like to take a seat. Gethin, get the man a coffee. He looks like he needs it.'

Ren's tone was mild but Skye could see a twinkle in his eye and knew that he was most likely enjoying himself.

She couldn't quite share his enjoyment, knowing what was coming next.

'How did you find out? Did you snoop around whilst I wasn't looking?'

Skye could feel her cheeks colour.

'Of course not!' She felt indignant at the suggestion and wasn't about to be cowed by the man's attitude. 'I overheard you and your wife speaking.'

She could feel her cheeks colour a little. That wasn't much better than snooping, except she hadn't intended to listen in.

'That's even worse! A private conversation between a man and his wife!'

'Perhaps it would be worth, in the future, considering who might overhear your conversation,' Ren said, again in the same mild tone. 'Skye was merely waiting for your man to drive her back here. She can't help it if she hears you speaking near an open window.' Ren winked at her and Skye gave him a grateful grimace.

'Anything you heard,' Raleigh said stressing the first word, 'would have been covered by client confidentiality.'

Skye swallowed — she knew this was coming and she also knew that Raleigh was right, at least in the legal sense.

'I agree,' Skye said, 'except in the case of business dealings that could be considered shady.'

She looked up from the study of her hands and looked Raleigh in the eye. She took comfort from the fact that he couldn't hold her gaze and had to look away.

'Everything I'm doing is legal. The source of the water is on my land and therefore I have the right to do with it what I will.'

'You are right, of course,' Skye said. 'Legally you can do as you please, but as a land owner you should know that is not the way things are done.'

'The only thing I am concerned about is the legality.'

'You might want to reconsider that,' Skye said, a thought suddenly coming to her. 'Land ownership is tough if you are alone. There is an unwritten code for land owners, in relation to doing what is best for the land, over and above what is best for the individual.'

Skye could only hope that this was not just a Scottish tradition. She didn't think it was. Surely it had to be true everywhere and Ren's subtle nod told her that she was right.

'Are you threatening me?' Raleigh's voice had risen half an octave.

'Not at all. Simply advising you on the ways of country life.'

'I don't need a committee to make decisions.' He sounded indignant.

'No, you don't, but a lack of consideration for your fellow land owners will come back to bite you in the future.'

'What could I possibly need from them?' Raleigh was contemptuous. And Skye knew what he was thinking — everything you needed could be overcome, if you had enough money.

'Money isn't the currency around here, Mr Raleigh; goodwill is.'

'I have spoken to your manager. I

think it would be safe to assume that you no longer have a job.' Raleigh raised an eyebrow, looking as if he expected her to be shocked.

'I would expect them to do nothing less,' Skye said, managing to hide any emotion she might be feeling.

'And you can expect to hear from my lawyers with regards to breach of a verbal contract.'

'That could be interesting,' Gethin said, sounding to Skye's ears remarkably calm. 'Since the information was overheard and not shared in a business context, I would be surprised if any judge would award you damages for failing to ensure your so-called private conversation was actually private.'

Skye was grateful that Gethin had stepped in. She had known she would lose her job, but if Raleigh decided to sue her she would need to get a solicitor herself, whether his case had merit or not, and it wasn't as if she had a pile of money in the bank saved.

'I have nothing more to say.' Raleigh

stood up abruptly and Ren followed suit, moving slowly on his bad knee and causing Raleigh's temper to be stretched further than it already was.

'I'll see myself out,' he barked.

Skye and Gethin sat in silence as the door slammed, followed by the sound of an engine being revved.

'He might want to see a doctor about his blood pressure,' Ren said, filling up his coffee mug.

Skye tried a weak smile.

'It will be fine, Skye. It's just bluster,' Gethin said.

'I'm sorry about your job, lass,' Ren said as he took his seat across from her.

'I knew that would happen. It's fine,' Skye said, even though she knew it wasn't.

What was she going to do now? She had a rented flat in London and bills to pay and no means to pay them.

'What can we do to help?' Gethin said anxiously.

'I think I probably need to go back to London,' Skye said.

She didn't want to go back to her office for what would be the last time — nor did she want to leave the farm.

'Of course, love. Gethin can take you out to that hire car of yours and see if he can get it back on the road. The weather's set to hold so you should have a clear run back.' Ren stood and rinsed his coffee mug in the sink. 'I don't think I can thank you enough for what you've done for us.' Ren said the words softly, whilst looking out of the kitchen window before turning to Skye.

Skye stood up and Ren pulled her into a tight hug.

'And I don't just mean the water,' he whispered softly. He released her and stood back so that he could see her face.

'Whatever you decide to do, you will always have a home here.' Ren's voice wobbled a bit as he said the words, then he leaned in and kissed her on the cheek before walking out of the kitchen and leaving Gethin and Skye alone.

'If you collect your things, I'll get the

truck out,' Gethin said, turning away from Skye. She reached out a hand to stop him.

'I have to go — you understand, don't you?'

Gethin didn't turn around but simply nodded.

'Of course. If I can't get the car started I'll drop you down to the village where you can get a bus into town.'

Skye watched him walk away from her, as Bryn walked up to her side and leaned in. She reached down and smoothed his fur.

'Maybe this is a good thing,' she whispered softly as Bryn whined.

It didn't sound like he agreed at all. She had thrown her life into a storm to do the right thing, but that didn't necessarily mean that Gethin and this farm was the right choice for her future. Perhaps being back in London would help her to figure that out.

22

Is Love Enough?

Skye hauled her suitcases down the stairs with difficulty. Firstly they were heavy, full of outfits that she had not worn and would probably never need to wear again, and secondly because Bryn seemed to think she was a sheep that needed shepherding.

When she got to the bottom of the stairs with the last suitcase, she could see through the open door. Gethin was standing by the old 60s-style truck. He had opened the passenger side door for her and when he had loaded in the last case, he climbed into the driving seat.

Gethin drove away from the farmhouse. The roads were still covered in compacted snow but Gethin seemed to know how to negotiate them.

'I'll call you and let you know when I

get back,' Skye said and then winced, remembering the whole phone situation. 'Sorry. I could write or maybe you could give me your dad's friend's number and he could radio you?'

'I don't have it on me,' Gethin said and Skye sighed.

She couldn't help it. Were they really going to go back to this, even after everything they had shared, all the things they had told each other about how they felt.

'Don't be like that,' Skye said. She knew it might be a red rag to a bull but she didn't think she could leave things as they were and Gethin's mood seemed set.

'I'm sorry, I don't have it with me.' And this time he sounded apologetic.

Skye reached out a hand for his, on the steering wheel. She felt him stiffen a little under her touch but he didn't shake her off.

'I do have to go. I need to return the hire car and speak to my boss.'

'I know.' His voice sounded quiet,

like a child who was being forced to agree with something that he didn't want to. 'I don't want you to,' he added and Skye smiled.

'I think we both need some space to think about what we want.'

'I know what I want,' Gethin said and turned his attention from the road to Skye's face. She could see a fierceness that scared her a little.

'Gethin, we have only known each other for a few days. What you are asking is for me to turn my back on everything in my life. I need time to think. We need time to work out how we feel and whether we want to see what might happen. I'm not sure we should rush things.'

Gethin nodded as they rounded a bend and came across the car.

'It's fine. I know how I feel, but you don't. You need to go away and think about it.'

Skye used the excuse of climbing out of the car, to hide her face and the emotions that she felt sure were written across it. She did love Gethin, she was sure of it. What she wasn't sure of, was whether that would be enough. The last thing she wanted to do was hurt him and it seemed that she had managed to do that, despite her best intentions.

Skye pulled the hire car keys from her shoulder bag and beeped the car unlocked. She climbed in and turned the key and the engine buzzed into life. Now all she had to do was free it from the snowdrift and then she could be on her way.

She put the car in reverse and was surprised when it moved relatively smoothly out of the snowdrift, which collapsed in a heap in the space where the car bonnet had been.

Gethin loaded her cases into the boot. He looked as if he was going to climb into the truck and drive off without a word, but seemed to change his mind at the last minute.

'I don't want you to go,' he said and reached for both of her hands, holding them tightly in his own.

'I don't have a choice, Gethin. Please understand. So much has happened and I need to work it all out in my head.'

'Can't you do that here?' His face looked so hopeful that Skye smiled sadly.

'Not with you to distract me, no — and besides, you need time to think too.'

He shook his head but then, seeing her face, he shrugged.

'If you say so.'

'I do. I'll be in touch,' she said and stood on her tiptoes to kiss his cheek.

'I'll hound the postman,' Gethin said. 'And maybe try and talk Dad into getting a phone installed.'

He smiled down at her and then pulled her into his arms, before kissing her as if he wouldn't see her for years. In that moment, Skye could feel her resolve buckle a little and so she was the first to break away.

'I love you,' Gethin said as she climbed into the hire car.

'I love you, too,' Skye said and closed the car door, needing a physical barrier between them for fear she would give in.

Skye allowed herself one glance in the rear-view mirror at Gethin's solitary figure as she pulled away and then forced herself to concentrate on the road, brushing away the tears that flowed down her cheeks.

When Skye reached the Severn crossing, she knew she had a decision to make. She could follow the M48 to join the M4 to London, or head north, the direction that her heart was telling her to go.

Her phone had been buzzing continuously as soon as the service returned but Skye had ignored it. She didn't need to read the texts, e-mails or phone messages to know what they said. None of that seemed to matter right now. What she needed to do was work out what she was going to do next and the only way she knew how to do that, was to head north.

Skye drove for four hours, until her stomach insisted that she stop. She pulled into a service station and made her way to the restaurant. She carried her tray of burger and chips to a window seat and reluctantly pulled out her phone.

The only person that she would have been pleased to hear from was the one person who had no way of contacting her and vice versa. She had cried most of the way through Wales, until it felt like she had no tears left.

The messages were exactly as she had expected. She had been fired and her boss had not minced words. Her belongings would be left in a box at reception, since she was not welcome back in the office. She would get no severance pay and none of the expenses of the trip would be covered.

Skye was almost relieved. At least her boss hadn't threatened to sue her as Mr Raleigh had, and picking up her belongings from reception would mean she wouldn't need to face any of her old colleagues, who would either be angry or bemused that she had thrown away such an opportunity.

Back in the car, she drove until her eyelids felt heavy and once again she left the road at a service station and booked herself into one of the roadside motels. She had thought she wouldn't be able to sleep, despite her fatigue, but her eyes closed as soon as her head hit the pillow and she didn't wake up till morning.

★ ★ ★

Looking at the map, Skye knew that she could reach her destination by lunch-time. She drove round the narrow lanes with practised ease, as though she had never been away. The countryside didn't seem to have changed, like it was frozen in time.

She drove up to the wooden gate that was closed across the lane which led up to the farm. Skye knew she couldn't go up there. She had no right, not any more. The land had been incorporated into a neighbouring farm, which in turn had been bought by a business, rather than a family. Skye wasn't sure what her dad had found most painful, the loss of the land or the fact that a way of life was ending.

So instead, she kept driving until she reached a lay-by. She drove the car into the lay-by and parked. Climbing out, she headed towards the small gate which would lead her to a path, which was a right of way.

The ground was uneven and pitted with stones but she kept climbing. Finally, she was at the highest point of the land which had once belonged to her family — the one place where she could see the whole farm, stretched out before her.

She sat on a rough wooden bench, one that her dad had built, in his favourite spot, and looked out across the land.

There were signs of change now, more machinery and some of the field boundaries had moved but she could still see her dad's handiwork. She could still feel her connection to the land. There was less pain with the emotion now, and she could think of her dad with only a few tears.

'I need to know what to do, Dad,' she whispered softly, as if he was sitting there beside her.

23

And Time Stood Still

The noise, the smells and the sheer volume of people made Skye feel like she had landed in a foreign land. It had taken her time to get used to, when she had first arrived, but quickly she found it comforting that not everyone knew your business, and quite frankly they didn't care to know. But being back, after her time away, she wondered that she had ever felt at home here. Standing on the steps to the office building where she had once worked, she felt as if she were remembering a past life.

Ten minutes later she was back outside, carrying a small cardboard box that contained everything personal she had taken to work, and it was a pitiful amount. One small photograph of her as a child with her dad, in a plain, white wooden frame. Not taken at the farm — she couldn't bear to look at those — but on a rare trip to Edinburgh, standing outside the castle on the hill.

A few stationery items and a strongly-worded letter reminding her that she was to have no contact with any of the clients that she had previous worked for. It almost made Skye laugh, that they were concerned she might try to poach some of their business.

It had been a challenge at first and so different from the rest of her life that she had relished it, but now she couldn't imagine herself back in an office, calling up suppliers to demand why the canapes hadn't arrived at the venue.

She had already told her flatmate all about it and said that she was going to have to leave London, since she couldn't afford to live there any more. Her flatmate had attempted to be understanding but it was clear that she was not best pleased.

Not that Skye could blame her, but she was starting to feel like there was no-one in her life right now who wasn't cross with her. What she still hadn't figured out was what she was going to do next.

The thoughts seemed to consume her and as she stepped off the last step and on to the pavement, she crashed into something solid. The cardboard box fell from her hands and the contents spilled over the pavement, punctured by the sound of breaking glass from the photo frame. Skye could feel herself start to fall but then hands reached out for her.

'Careful!' a voice said, in an accent that was instantly recognisable.

Skye couldn't bring herself to look up, since she was sure she was imagining it and the person she had bumped into would be just another Londoner.

'Skye?' His voice seemed less sure now, as if he was wondering if he had made a mistake.

She looked up and her heart danced. It was him.

'What are you doing here?' she asked.

'I know you said you needed time and space but I've been going crazy ... ' Gethin didn't seem to know how to put how it felt into words. 'I needed to see you.'

'How did you find me?'

'I got Lewis to look up your company on his computer and then I just sort of waited here, hoping you would turn up.'

Skye blinked and then stared.

'How long have you been here?' she asked incredulously.

'I was here all day yesterday.' He smiled at her uncertainly.

'What about the farm and your dad?'

'He said I was no use to him, moping about.'

Now Gethin looked like he wished he hadn't been quite so honest and Skye couldn't help but smile.

Gethin bent down and picked up the broken frame, picking out the pieces of broken glass and placing it carefully back into the box, before picking up a few stray pens and a notebook.

'I can't believe you came all this way to find me,' Skye said.

'I was worried that you would demand I went straight back home. I just had to know you were OK. Normally I'm happy that we don't have a phone or a mobile signal but the last few days, I've been wishing it was different.'

'Me too,' Skye said shyly and was rewarded with a huge grin.

'I know you have stuff to work out and I promise I'll give you the time to do that. I just needed to see you. Now I have, I'll head back.'

Gethin turned to walk away and Skye reached out and grabbed his arm.

'Oh, no, you don't, mister.'

'Seriously, Skye, I've left Da to it for two days already. I really should go.' His words were serious and sensible but he seemed unable to keep the grin from his lips.

'I have something I want to say first.'

Gethin's smile slipped a little and his eyes creased with worry. Skye opened her mouth to speak but no words would come, so instead, she got up on her tiptoes and kissed him. When their lips touched, Skye felt a spark cross between them and she knew that Gethin felt it, too. His arms encircled her and time stood still.

'What was it that you wanted to say?' Gethin finally asked, clearly reluctant to break off the kiss.

'I think that just about sums it up,' Skye said, feeling strangely shy. 'I love you,' she added softly, as they were getting curious glances from the people walking past.

'I love you too,' Gethin said, 'but I think we had established that before you left.' His face was serious again and Skye wondered if she could detect a little reproach in his voice.

'I didn't mean that quite like it sounded. It's just I know that you need time and space and I haven't really given you that.' He ruffled his hair with his hand and Skye had to bite her lip to keep from smiling. 'What I'm trying to say, badly, is that I respect you need time and space. What I'm asking from you is huge, I know that, and so I want you to take all the time you need.'

Skye opened her mouth to speak. She knew what she wanted to say now. She thought she had probably always known, since the moment she first met him. Skye didn't get a chance to utter any of the words aloud, as Gethin had pressed a finger to her lips.

'I'm going back home and if you let me have your address, I will write, every day. And I will wait. Wait until you are sure you know what you want.' He seemed to swallow with effort. 'And if that's not me, then I will respect your decision.'

Skye tried to speak again but Gethin shook his head and she held her tongue.

'If it is me, well, you know where to find me.'

Skye was about to tell him what she

had decided but he silenced her once again with a kiss.

'Now, Miss Mackenzie, if you are free, will you direct me to Paddington train station? I would be most grateful.'

'I'll do better than that. I will escort you personally.' She slipped her hand into his and led the way to the nearby tube station.

It made her love him more that he had taken on board what she had said she needed, and was now insisting that she stick to it.

Waving Gethin off at the station had been one of the hardest things that Skye had ever had to do. She would see Gethin again, she was sure of it. She knew now what she wanted. She had some things she needed to do first, but once they were done, only wild horses could keep her away.

24

With This Ring . . .

Gethin had been true to his word, and every day a letter had arrived at the flat that she still shared. She had written back, too, but hers had been briefer. She didn't want to give away her big surprise.

Skye had sold or given away most of her belongings so all that she owned now were two suitcases full of clothes and a box of books and photographs.

The things that she had bought, that she had thought she needed, didn't make her happy any more. Skye knew now that she had been trying to be someone that she wasn't but all that was about to change.

She smiled as she reached the Severn bridge. She hadn't told Gethin she was coming. She had told him that she loved him many times but given away no hint of her plans.

Skye could feel the nerves a little now. There had been nothing in his letters to suggest that he had changed his mind or that his feelings had lessened, still, it felt like a risk all the same — but it also felt like the only choice she could make.

It was four more hours until Skye found herself in the nearest village to Gethin and Ren's farm. All she wanted to do was drive straight there and run into his arms but she needed to do this first, and so she took a right hand turn instead of a left and drove up to the front of The Manor.

She climbed out of the car and walked up to the small site office, which was housed in what was once the gatehouse.

'Miss Mackenzie,' Mr Raleigh said, but this time there was none of the effusive greeting that there had been at their first meeting. 'I have to admit that I was surprised to receive your call.'

'Thank you for agreeing to hear my proposal,' Skye said, holding out a hand. Raleigh inspected it for a moment and then shook it.

'You appreciate, I'm sure, that I have decided not to go with your company.'

'I am no longer employed, Mr Raleigh, so I can assure you I am not here to bid for your business.'

Raleigh eyed her warily for a moment and then held out an arm to direct her towards the office. He took his seat first, a large, black leather, executive chair and Skye took the seat opposite his wide desk.

'I am a busy man. Perhaps you can tell me what you came here to say.'

Skye took a deep breath and looked him in the eye.

'Firstly, I would like to apologise for my actions and for any issues they may have caused you.' She was also thankful that he had decided against suing her but thought that was probably not a good thing to mention at this juncture.

'Whilst I appreciate your words, your

actions cost me time and money. Not to mention, shall we say, some problems with the neighbours.'

Skye nodded.

'That is what I would like to speak with you about. I have a proposal which I think will meet everyone's needs.'

Raleigh arched an eyebrow but he was clearly not convinced.

Skye had spent several weeks on the proposal. She had paid an engineer, with the last of her savings, to draw up the plans and all she could do now was wait for Raleigh's response. He flicked through the document that she had put together.

'Whilst I admit that this is an interesting proposal, I think you will understand that I will need my own team of experts to look it over to ensure it is a viable option.'

'Of course.'

'But before I do that, let me speak plainly.'

Skye remained silent, sure he had never done anything but.

'What do you expect to gain from this? If it is money, then . . . '

Skye waved his words away.

'I see it as recompense for my actions. I'm not asking for anything other than for you to consider it as an option.'

'An option that would smooth relations with neighbouring farms and give the locals what they want?' Raleigh's voice was a little brittle but Skye was certain he was at least considering what she had suggested.

'An added benefit for you, surely?' Skye said looking him squarely in the eye.

'It would certainly get the Farmers' Union off my back.' He steepled his hands together and stared openly at Skye and she held his gaze. 'Very well, I will ask my man to look at it. And if,' he stressed the word, 'it is viable and cost effective then, well, we will see.'

Skye knew it was as much as she could hope for. She stood up and held out her hand.

'Thank you for your time.'

Raleigh nodded, still studying her.

'You have a lively business mind, Miss Mackenzie.'

Skye thought he was going to say something more but when he remained silent, she decided that now would be a good time to leave.

Back in the car, the last few miles seemed to take longer than the whole journey put together. It was almost four o'clock when she pulled into the farmyard and she was a little disappointed that it was deserted. No doubt, Ren and Gethin were out somewhere working.

Skye wasn't worried. She knew the front door was never locked and so let herself in, before heading to the kitchen, carrying the bags of food she had picked up at the small village post office and set about making dinner.

'Hello?' a voice said, both curious and hopeful.

'I'm in the kitchen!' Skye called but she couldn't keep the grin from her face as Gethin practically ran to her and scooped her up into his arms.

He spun her round several times and then set her feet back on the ground and pulled her into a kiss. The kiss carried on until Ren cleared his throat and they broke apart, slightly breathless and pink cheeked.

'Lass, I told him it were you but he said it could be anyone.'

Skye threw her arms around Ren's neck and kissed him on the cheek.

'Just popped in for a visit, did you?' Ren asked, but his face was lit by a cheeky grin.

Skye's eyes found Gethin's.

'Longer, if you'll have me?'

'For ever?' Gethin said and Skye nodded and they stared at each other, like they had said everything that was important.

'Well, get on with it, lad. We have more work to do after supper.'

Ren's words seemed to cut through the dream state that Gethin was in and he nodded distractedly before getting down on one knee.

Skye's eyes went wide as Gethin fished in his pocket for something. Not finding it, he searched another.

'You'd better not have lost it, lad, or your mother will return to haunt you.'

Gethin pulled a thin band of gold, with a tiny diamond laid into it, from his pocket and showed it first to his dad before holding out to Skye.

'Skye Mackenzie? I know we've only known each other for a short while but would you do me the honour of . . . '

'Yes!' Skye said, trying to blink back tears.

'I haven't asked it yet!' Gethin said indignantly. 'I've been practising it for weeks.'

'Aye, and no sheep has said yes yet,' Ren said drily, 'but I think you can take that as a yes, can't he, love?'

Skye laughed and found herself once again in Gethin's arms, once she had been thoroughly hugged and kissed. Ren stepped in and threw his arms around both of them.

'What did I tell you?' Ren said and Gethin rolled his eyes.

'Yes, Da. You were right, as always.'

'And don't you forget it.'

A shrill bell sound broke the happy silence.

'What's that?' Skye said, wondering if they had some sort of alarm on the outbuildings.

'Come with me,' Gethin said and led her to the lounge, where on a table sat a telephone.

'You've got a phone?'

'Aye, lass, it's one thing for us to live out here with limited means of contact but Gethin seemed to think you would be happier being able to ring people without having to climb the hill to get a signal.'

Skye turned to Gethin, who shrugged.

'I just thought . . . ' His voice trailed off. Skye knew exactly what he thought and she could have kissed him for it. So she did.

'Answer it, then,' Ren said in mock impatience.

'Hello?' Gethin said, as if it was the first time he had answered a phone.

'Oh, right, yes, he's right here,' Gethin held the phone out to his dad. 'It's David, from the Farmers' Union.'

Gethin took Skye by the hand and led her back into the kitchen. He sat down on the bench seat and pulled her into his arms.

'I wonder what that's about?' Gethin said, his face creasing into a frown.

Skye kissed his forehead and the frown was gone.

'What?' he asked, seeing the look in her eye.

She shrugged as if to say 'nothing' but his suspicious look told her that he wasn't fooled.

'You never did, lass?' Ren said walking into the kitchen. Skye's eyes were wide and her fingers crossed, she hoped she knew what Ren was going to say. Gethin looked from his dad to Skye and then back to his dad.

'Did what?' Gethin was impatient now.

'David said that Raleigh chap has been in touch with a new proposal. One that will mean he'll get his moat and we'll keep our water. Not only that but he's reconsidered and wants to use local produce at the castle.'

Ren stared at Skye, somewhat dazed.

'You did this?' Gethin asked her and she nodded, eyes locked on his.

'I needed to make it right, for him and for us.'

'Us? Now that I like the sound of.' Gethin shook his head. 'If I know you a lifetime I have a feeling that you'll still be able to surprise me.'

Skye kissed him gently on the lips.

'I should hope so, lad,' Ren said softly, 'that's what love is all about. Now then, who wants a cuppa to celebrate?'

THE LEGACY OF BLACKTHORN

June Davies

During a stormy winter's night, Meirian Penlan travels by stage-coach to take up a mysterious post at Blackthorn Manor. Wild and remote, Blackthorn lies amongst the great meres of Lancashire, surrounded by long-held superstitions, tales of witchcraft and uncanny occurrences. Once there, Meirian is drawn into a web of scandal, deception, blackmail and tragedy. Discovering old love letters and a terrible secret, she risks everything to set right a dreadful wrong — and unravel the disappearance of Blackthorn's medieval jewels . . .